WHERE WE BELONG

TETON MOUNTAIN SERIES
BOOK 1

KELLIE COATES GILBERT

For Justice Nicole and Skylar. You are family to me.

PRAISE FOR KELLIE COATES GILBERT NOVELS

"If you're looking for a new author to read, you can't go wrong with Kellie Coates Gilbert." ~**Lisa Wingate**, NY Times bestselling author of *Before We Were Yours*

"Well-drawn, sympathetic characters and graceful language ~**Library Journal**

"Deft, crisp storytelling" ~**RT Book Reviews**

"I devoured the book in one sitting."~**Chick Lit Central**

"Gilbert's heartfelt fiction is always a pleasure to read." ~**Buzzing About Books**

"Kellie Coates Gilbert delivers emotionally gripping plots and authentic characters." ~**Life Is Story**

"I laughed, I cried, I wanted to throw my book against the wall, but I couldn't quit reading." ~**Amazon reader**

WHERE WE BELONG

TETON MOUNTAIN SERIES, BOOK 1

Kellie Coates Gilbert

1

C harlie Grace leaned forward and focused on her reflection in the high school bathroom mirror. "Did either of you bring hairspray?"

Lila shook her head. "No, but your hair looks great."

"You need a little more volume in those bangs," Reva acknowledged. She pulled a can of Aqua Net from her Jordache purse and handed it over. "Good thing I came prepared."

Charlie Grace took the can. "You're amazing." She ratted the front of her fawn-colored bob a bit more, then held the can in place and sent a spray of product across the top of her head. She grabbed her graduation cap. "Now, how is this supposed to go?"

Reva stepped forward. "Here, I'll do it for you. If this black girl knows anything, it's fashion accessories."

"Help me with mine, too?" Lila asked, holding her cap against her own dark hair.

The bathroom door suddenly flew open. In rushed Capri, long blonde hair flying, and her dress and gown draped over one arm. "Am I late?"

"Oh my gosh, why do you do this?" Reva asked. "Hurry and change. The procession starts in less than fifteen minutes."

Reva pinned Charlie Grace's cap in place, then lifted her friend's hand to examine her new engagement ring. Although the stone was petite, it was pretty. "I still can't believe we're graduating. And you're getting married soon."

Capri unbuttoned her jeans and kicked off her boots. "Me either."

A wistful look filled Lila's face. "You know, everything is about to change. I mean, soon, Reva will be heading off to Tulane. Charlie Grace will be a married woman. I'm starting vet school." She turned to Capri. "And..."

Capri waved off her nostalgia. "Guys, who cares about the future?" she said with a devilish grin. "Let's just enjoy today, celebrate our hard work, and worry about the rest later."

Like Lila, Charlie Grace couldn't help but feel a sense of impending change. She gave one last glance in the mirror. "It went by so fast. Everything is about to be different."

Reva parked her hands on her hips. "Not everything. Thunder Mountain has remained the same ever since I moved here. I mean, after we have diplomas in hand, do you really think this tiny mountain town will be any different? They'll still be grilling hamburgers and serving beer down at the Rustic Pine. The shelves at Western Drug and General will still be stocked with green beans and corn. Mrs. Cavendish will continue spreading gossip every chance she gets."

She held out her hand and caught Capri's jeans as she flung them aside. "The doors to this high school will open next fall, and another couple of dozen kids will start freshman algebra with Mr. Jolley. More pimple-faced fourteen-year-old boys will learn to build engines in shop class with Mr. Reay. The doors of Moose Chapel will open on Sunday mornings. Summers will be filled with tourists hoping to spot a bear or a moose. They'll all leave when the quaking aspen leaves start turning. As I said, some things never change."

"But we will," Lila argued.

Capri slipped her gown over her head and said in a muffled voice. "Things will change only if we want them to."

Undeterred, Lila turned to her friends with tears in her eyes. "I know we'll all be going our separate ways," she said, "but we're going to stay friends forever, right?"

Charlie Grace rushed to her side. "Of course, we will," she insisted, reassuring Lila with a tight hug. "Nothing could ever tear us apart."

"Besides, I won't stay in New Orleans. I'll be back," Reva told them with firm insistence. "We'll always be here for each other," she added, taking Capri's hand. "It's where we belong."

2

Twenty years later

Charlie Grace pulled the worn leather glove from her hand and wiped her brow with her forearm. Even at this early hour, beads of sweat formed as she heaved hay bales from the barn and carried them to the feeding pen.

"This isn't my job," she muttered out loud. "Not when I pay someone good money to work." She let the bale tumble at her feet and pulled the pocketknife from her jeans pocket. She opened it cautiously, taking care not to slice her finger, then slid the sharp blade across the yellow twine, releasing the hay into the splintered wooden trough. Dusty dried alfalfa leaves blew up into her face.

She coughed and pulled her inhaler from her other pocket. Lifting the small plastic contraption to her mouth, she drew a long, airy pull of the medicine and tried not to growl as she shoved the thing back inside her pocket.

Charlie Grace worked with haste, knowing she had to get

the cattle fed and return to the house. The school bus showed up each day promptly at seven-thirty sharp. If Jewel wasn't at the end of their ranch lane waiting, she'd miss her ride to school, and Charlie Grace would have to drive her daughter into town. She didn't have time for that today.

Not when she had an important meeting with Reva and the bankers this morning.

One of the heifers lifted its head from the trough and stared.

"I hope this isn't an indication of how this day is going to go," Charlie Grace told the young Angus. "And don't go batting those long eyelashes. Your turn will come once breeding season hits. You'll see how challenging it is to maneuver life with an offspring who needs everything from you." She tilted her head toward the neighboring pen. "And don't go thinking any of those steers will help. All they do is eat and breed." She slapped her glove on the leg of her jeans. "You'd be doing good to remember that."

Charlie Grace pulled on her gloves and headed toward the house, taking in the majestic mountain peaks in the distance and savoring their beauty.

Overhead, the sky was changing shades, from the pretty orange sherbet of dawn to early morning robin-egg blue. Charlie Grace took a deep breath of crisp air filled with the scent of sagebrush and pine needles before letting her attention drift to the far end of the pine meadow, where a herd of elk headed in the direction of the large creek that wound through their Wyoming property.

This never got old.

Teton Trails Ranch was her home, the only home she'd known. These acres of land fed her soul, no matter what kind of day she seemed to be having.

That thought brought a whistle to her lips as she made her way past the newly constructed guest cabins to the log ranch house. Two border collies remained close at her feet as she reached her destination and climbed the steps onto the porch. Smiling, she reached inside her jeans pocket and tossed them each a dog biscuit.

Her dad sat in his wheelchair next to the far railing with a cup of steaming coffee. "You're late. Where you been?"

Charlie Grace was startled by the gruffness in his voice. "Morning, Dad." She braced for what she knew would come when she admitted where she'd been. "I had to feed this morning."

"Thought we had a ranch hand for that."

"Well...he was a no-show this morning."

"Didn't I tell you that Roy Mullins wouldn't last? You should have listened to me. All those boys from Cheyenne care about is their rodeo and whiskey."

Charlie Grace steeled herself, unable to let his comment go. "You rode bulls on the circuit, Dad." She refrained from mentioning his love for whiskey.

He huffed. "Yeah? Well, no more."

She stiffened. "Dad, I don't have time for this. I've got to get Jewel to the bus stop."

He growled and waved her off before maneuvering his wheelchair so his back was to her.

Gritting her teeth, she headed inside.

"Hello, sweetheart." Aunt Mo was standing at the sink, washing dishes. "You have that big meeting today, so I thought I'd drop over and help out a bit. Jewel is brushing her teeth."

"You're a godsend," Charlie Grace told her as she kissed her aunt's weathered cheek.

"Your breakfast is on the table, dear."

Charlie Grace opened her mouth to protest.

Aunt Mo raised her soapy hand in the air. "Nuh-uh. You sit and eat. You can't abuse your body and starve it of proper nutrition, or it'll soon give out on you."

She had a point. Doing as she was told, she picked up the fork and filled her mouth with scrambled eggs, still warm. She chewed while standing, then swallowed and washed the food down with a swig of orange juice.

Maureen Rivers, as she was known to everyone else, was one of the fittest women in Thunder Mountain...even at nearly seventy. She had a spunk for life that Charlie Grace could only wish for. Despite life's setbacks, the woman found a way to exhibit joy and happiness. She claimed she wanted nothing more than what the good Lord determined to give her each day. That was enough.

"Hi, Mom. Don't forget, I need money for the book fair."

Charlie Grace turned to see her daughter standing with her backpack heaved over her shoulder. Her long auburn hair was braided down the back. From the looks of the strands sticking out, she'd styled it herself.

"Come here, honey. I didn't forget." She pointed to the envelope on the counter with her daughter's name scribbled across the front and motioned Jewel closer.

"What?"

Without answering, Charlie Grace turned her daughter around and pulled the band from the bottom of the braid. "Excellent try, but you left some hanging loose. Let me fix it for you."

Jewel tugged away. "I can do it."

"Honey, we don't have time. Please, let me help." The look she gave her daughter messaged that she wasn't taking no for an answer.

Charlie Grace couldn't help but smile. Jewel was just like her at that age. Before her mother died, she wouldn't allow her mom to give her assistance with anything. Like Jewel, she was independent and not about to let others intercede...especially when her mom wanted to place those pink foam curlers in her hair the night before school pictures. Like she wanted to be called a curly-headed ninny by the red-headed boy who sat behind her and poked her with pencils in class.

That boy turned out to be her husband. She should clarify...ex-husband. The uncomfortable pokes in the back were nothing compared to the women he'd not-so-secretly poked over their entire marriage.

Even with the disdain she still held for him, Gibbs Nichols had given her the best thing in her entire life...Jewel. While sharing parental duties—and that was a stretch of her patience—she was grateful he still wanted to be in his daughter's life.

Father-daughter relationships were important. They shaped how a girl thought of herself.

A banging at the door drew all their attention. "Girl! Let me in," her dad shouted.

Aunt Mo gave her a sympathetic glance before scurrying to open the door. She wiped her hands on a towel and turned the knob. "Settle down, Clancy. We're coming."

Charlie Grace tossed the brush on the kitchen table and turned Jewel around for a brief inspection. "Okay, you're good."

She grabbed her daughter's hand and pulled her toward the door, taking care to make a wide swath around her father.

"But, my money," Jewel protested.

Aunt Mo hurried and slipped the envelope into Jewel's waiting hands. "There you go, sweetheart." She took the little girl's chin in her hand. "Who's Aunt Mo's precious pudding gift of God?"

Her daughter's face drew into a wide grin. "I am." She reached and pulled at Aunt Mo's hand until the older woman leaned down. Jewel planted a big kiss on Aunt Mo's cheek, then moved for her grandfather and did the same.

While he grunted at the gesture, the corners of his lips lifted into a smile.

Charlie Grace and Jewel scrambled across the porch and

down the stairs, then hurried for the long dirt drive. Before they could reach the end of the lane, the bus honked.

Charlie Grace waved frantically. "Wait, we're coming!"

The door on the bus opened. "Take your time," Donna Hatfield hollered. "I'm running early today."

Despite the extended courtesy, Charlie Grace and Jewel both broke into a full sprint. At the bus, Charlie Grace bent and kissed the top of her little girl's head. "Be good for your teacher today."

"I always am, Mom," Jewel assured her.

"And...be happy," Charlie Grace added wistfully. She watched her daughter climb the stairs onto the bus and wave back at her. The bus door closed.

She drew a slow breath and closed her eyes. "It's important that you be happy."

3

W ith barely a greeting, Charlie Grace hurried past Carol Deegan at the reception desk inside the Thunder Mountain Bank and Trust office and headed directly for the conference room where her friend, Reva, and Mr. Cavendish were waiting.

Despite her best efforts to arrive on time, her drive into town had been delayed when a small black bear darted out from the trees and ran directly into the small car in front of her. She'd had no choice but to stop and jump out. The bear didn't appear injured and shook off the stunned look on its face before it jumped up and darted back into the trees, not even limping.

The man and woman inside the car climbed slowly out in bewilderment. "What just happened?" the driver asked.

The woman stood with the passenger door open, her hand on her chest. "Did we just hit something?"

"A bear," Charlie Grace told them. "It ran out of the pines and hit your back tire."

The wide-eyed woman glanced around. "Where is it?"

Charlie Grace pointed to the tree-covered hillside. "Up

there. Wasn't bleeding or limping, so I don't think the animal was injured significantly. Just a bit dazed."

The driver raced to his back tire. "I hope there's no damage. This is a rental."

"I don't see any," the woman confirmed after inspecting the rear end of their car.

Charlie Grace checked her watch. "Look, I have a meeting and need to go. But you are both okay, right?"

They nodded.

"Okay, well...enjoy the rest of your vacation." Charlie Grace hurried back to her farm truck and climbed inside. She started the engine and punched the gas pedal, hoping Fleet Southcott wasn't parked on the edge of town with his radar gun, waiting to pull over anyone who dared to speed through their small town.

Luckily, Fleet's police car was parked outside the Rustic Pine, where he was likely enjoying some bacon and eggs with a few of his cronies, leaving her free to make it to her destination without further interruption.

As Charlie Grace approached the bank's conference room, she paused and took a deep breath before opening the door. "Sorry, I'm late."

After shutting the conference door behind her, Charlie Grace tossed her purse on top of the long, polished table. "It's not even noon, and it's already been a day." She quickly told them about the incident with the bear.

"Wow," Reva said, her eyes wide. "That doesn't happen every day."

"Want some coffee?" Wooster Cavendish offered.

Charlie Grace slipped into a seat at the table. "No thanks."

Reva gave her an encouraging smile. "Well, let's get started. I have looked over the loan papers. With a few adjustments, I think we're now good to go."

Wooster tugged at his tie, which hung loose at his unbuttoned shirt collar. "Your attorney drives a hard bargain. Reva's quite the negotiator."

Charlie Grace suspected the bank manager didn't make a huge fuss when Reva wanted changes to the loan papers. He was known for being a softy. It was his meddlesome wife you had to look out for. Nicola Cavendish was known for having a lot of opinions she never resisted sharing.

Unexpected pressure built inside Charlie Grace's chest as Reva offered her a pen. "Are you ready?" Reva asked.

She swallowed. "I guess so."

Reva sensed her reticence. She reached and covered Charlie Grace's hand with her own. "You can do this. The guest ranch is going to be a smashing success. You've already done the hard part with the construction loan. This perm loan finalizes everything and provides the operating funds you'll need to open the doors and move forward." She glanced over at Wooster, who nodded in agreement. "We're all here to support you."

Charlie Grace gazed into the eyes of her good friend for strength. She swallowed and managed a smile. Steeling herself, she took the pen and stared down at the package of papers flagged with yellow tabs. "I'm ready."

Despite her resolve, her hands shook as she signed all twenty-seven places in the loan documentation. She scribbled her name on the final tabbed page—Charlotte Grace Rivers—and set the pen down.

"There. All done."

"Good girl." Reva slid the documents over to Mrs. Deegan, who had entered the room without Charlie Grace noticing, notary stamp in hand.

She leaned back against her chair. "That's it?"

"That's it," Reva told her. She stood and motioned for Charlie Grace to do the same. "I have a little surprise for you... or, I should say, *we* have a surprise."

Her good friend led her out of the bank onto the wooden plank sidewalk.

There stood her two other best friends—Lila Bellamy and Capri Jacobs. Capri held a huge bunch of helium balloons. Lila had a bouquet of flowers, not the ones they normally plucked from the meadows, but a stunning floral arrangement in a beautiful rustic vase that perfectly fit her taste.

"They're from Bear Country Gifts," Lila announced. "They ordered the pink and white hydrangeas in special."

"They're beautiful," Charlie Grace murmured.

"Congratulations," the girls said in unison.

"We're so proud of you," Lila said.

Charlie Grace wasn't surprised at this show of support. The four of them had been the closest of friends in school and had remained so.

As promised, Reva moved back to Thunder Mountain as soon as she had her law degree in hand. Still single, she lived alone in a custom-built cabin with a large deck overlooking the river. Her closet was nearly the size of Charlie Grace's entire bedroom. That didn't even include the space for Reva's collection of Jimmy Choo shoes.

Lila and her teenage daughter lived at the other end of town. Like Charlie Grace, she was a single mom. When she was six months pregnant, her husband of less than a year had been tragically killed in a helicopter crash in Fallujah.

She currently worked with Doc Tillman down at the veterinary clinic, which was perfect given her love of anything soft and furry. Despite all that she juggled, Lila was back in school, pursuing a large animal veterinarian license with a specialty in horses. "Camille's college fund needs a bit of help," she claimed. "I need the money the extra certification will provide." Never mind the fact that she was nearly killing herself in the process.

Capri Jacobs still lived with her parents. When questioned

about the decision, she shrugged. "It's free." The rest of them knew full well that money was not the deciding factor. Capri owned Grand Teton Whitewater Adventures. She killed it financially, especially during the heavy tourist season. Her chosen profession also left her free in the winters when she alternated filling her time with binging seasons of *Gilmore Girls* on television and snowmobile racing on the local circuit.

Wild adventures aside, Capri was dedicated to protecting her mother, who had married a man who tended to get a bit mean when he drank. Her mother's well-being was paramount —even to the point of Capri turning down multiple marriage proposals. Thankfully, as her stepfather aged, lemonade had finally replaced the glass of bourbon in the old man's hand.

Despite the twists and turns life had tossed their way, the four remained staunch supporters of one another and the best of friends. It was no surprise to see them standing in front of her, ready to help her celebrate.

Reva looped her arm in Charlie Grace's. "We have another surprise."

"We aren't meeting for breakfast?"

Capri shook her head. "Not this morning."

Lila pointed to Charlie Grace's pickup. "Get in and follow us."

"Where are we going?"

Reva beamed. "You'll see."

The destination turned out to be Teton Trails Ranch. As Charlie Grace maneuvered the final bend on the familiar dirt road, she glanced down at her phone to see a text message on the screen.

Surprise!

Charlie Grace looked up and nearly choked. At the entrance into the long winding lane leading to the house and barns stood a massive wooden gate her father had erected long before Charlie Grace could even remember. A crane perched feet away, lifting a large wooden sign into position on the upper cross beam. A man on the ground in an orange safety vest waved to a couple of other men perched in a hydraulic bucket ready to fasten the wooden placard into place.

The sign read: *TETON TRAILS GUEST RANCH.*

Charlie Grace's eyes filled with tears. She pulled the truck to the side of the road and cut the engine. With the back of her hand, she wiped her face and glanced in the rearview mirror, trying to collect her composure.

Taking a deep breath, she climbed from her truck. "What is this?"

Her three best friends ran to her side, radiating with broad smiles. "Are you surprised?" Capri asked.

Charlie Grace's hand went to her chest. "Shocked is more like it. How did you...why did you—"

Reva drew her into a shoulder hug. "It's our gift to you. Charlotte Grace Rivers, the proud owner of the best guest ranch within a hundred miles of the Tetons."

"Well, me and my dad. I mean, technically...."

Reva brushed off her comments with a wave of her hand. "The ranch is in a trust now. You manage the trust."

"That's not all," Capri blurted. She motioned to Lila, who pulled a laptop from the briefcase bag hanging from her shoulder. She opened the computer and set it on Charlie Grace's pickup bed.

After a few clicks of the keyboard, a beautiful image of the ranch with the Teton Mountain Range in the background appeared on the screen. "Voila!" Lila said, grinning from ear to ear.

Reva peered over their shoulders. "It's your new website. It will be no time at all before visitors to our area will be flocking to have the experience of their lifetime...right here at Teton Trails."

Capri clapped her hands with excitement. "Included is the

latest in online reservation systems. You are state of the art now, Charlie Grace."

Once again, Charlie Grace could barely breathe. A website was on her long list of things she had to get done before the opening, but she was technologically challenged, so she'd let the job fall to the bottom of her tasks. "I can't believe you guys did this." She turned, tears brimming once again. "You are the absolute best."

She drew her girlfriends into a hug. "Thank you doesn't seem enough."

And it wasn't.

It would take time to fully absorb how she'd been surrounded by friends who'd given her a glimmer of hope. Despite the obstacles ahead, perhaps the future might, indeed, be bright. Regardless, these women would not leave her side.

The Teton Trails Guest Ranch was scheduled to open in less than two weeks. A skeleton crew had been hired, and food and supplies ordered. She would do everything in her power to make the enterprise a success...and earn every ounce of this support.

If she were lucky, she'd also gain her father's respect, although that notion was a stretch. She'd likely be more apt to land on the moon.

4

———

C harlie Grace pulled her truck into the yard at the ranch house, filled with elation. Sure, she remained overwhelmed and nervous. There was a lot on the line. Yet her girlfriends' enthusiasm had gone a long way in helping her see the cup half full. Absolutely, there was a risk. There was also a good chance this endeavor would be a success...or at least hit near that benchmark.

She cut the engine and grabbed her purse, along with the folder containing a duplicate set of the signed loan papers.

The truth was, some of her elation could be attributed to the bottle of champagne Reva uncorked when the sign was finally in place. As soon as the equipment lumbered back down the road, the girls insisted on offering up a toast. Then, they'd insisted on taking her photo in front of the gate. "It's for the website," Lila insisted.

Charlie Grace smiled again, pushing the door open and heading into the house.

"What was all that damned commotion out at the gate?" her father demanded the minute she entered the kitchen.

"Oh, Clancy," Aunt Mo admonished, wiping her hands on a towel. "Language."

He ignored his sister. "Why all the equipment?"

In turn, Charlie Grace ignored him. "What are you still doing here, Aunt Mo? I thought your pinochle club was this afternoon?"

"It is, dear. But I wanted to get a casserole started for you." She pointed to the oven door. "The dish should be ready shortly. Mac and cheese with chunks of ham and a little diced jalapeño—not a lot, just a dab for flavor. You can heat it up later tonight for dinner."

Charlie Grace leaned and kissed her aunt's cheek. "Thank you. I don't know how to keep thanking you for all you do."

Aunt Mo drew her into a hug. "No thanks needed, sweetheart."

Her aunt released her grip and grabbed her purse from the counter before moving for the back door. With her hand on the knob, she turned and pointed at her brother. "You be nice." She winked in Charlie Grace's direction and left, closing the door behind her.

"Well, are you going to answer me? What was all that equipment down there?"

Charlie Grace sat at the kitchen table and pulled off her cowboy boots. "They set a sign on the gate leading into the ranch."

Her father huffed at her from his wheelchair. "What kind of sign?"

She lifted her chin slightly. "Teton Trails Guest Ranch."

Her father's eyes darkened. "Mo tells me you signed the loan paperwork today." He stared at her with contempt.

"Dad, we've been over this a thousand times. I know you don't like it, but I don't have a choice. This ranch is going broke for all the reasons we've discussed on more than one occasion."

"Oh, here we go. You think I drove this operation into the

ground. That an old man like me didn't know what he was doing." He jabbed his finger at her. "Listen here, sister. Ranching ain't for the faint of heart. We've weathered worse on more occasions than you can know. That's when you pick yourself up and work harder. Things always come back around."

"Not this time, Dad. And you're wrong. I don't blame you. The cash flow simply wasn't there. We had no way of meeting expenses." Charlie Grace groaned inside. Despite promising herself she wouldn't have this conversation with him yet again, he'd pulled her into hashing out her reasons all over again. "Dad, your accident changed everything. You know that. I'm doing the best I know how. You're going to have to trust me."

"If trusting you means turning this ranch into a glorified hotel for rich families and their brat children, then no thanks." He locked his gaze upon her. "Your grandfather, who homesteaded this place and built it from nothing...well, he'd turn over in his grave."

The intended barb hit its mark. She winced with the sting of it.

Before this conversation blew up into another heated exchange, Charlie Grace reminded herself there was no winning him over. For her sanity, she had to ignore the insults he continued to throw her way. She loved her father, but he could turn a cupcake into a pickle. She wasn't about to eat what he dished out tonight.

Instead, she'd focus on the few things she could control.

"Are you hungry, Dad?" She went for the cupboard and set the table, knowing he watched her. "Jewel should be home at any time. She had 4-H club, and Annie Cumberland promised to drive her home for me."

As if on cue, the sounds of a car on gravel pulled her attention to the kitchen window. "Looks like they're here."

Minutes later, Jewel came bounding through the door. "Hi, Mom! Guess what? 4-H camp will be only a few weeks after my birthday this summer. The cut-off is ten. I'll be old enough this year!" She ran and wrapped her arms around Charlie Grace's waist. "Can I go, Mom? Huh, can I?"

Charlie Grace had no way of promising that. At least not right now, not when so many expenses related to the opening were looming. "We'll see, honey." She ruffled the top of her daughter's head. "Go wash your hands. Dinner is nearly ready."

She turned her attention to the woman standing at the door. "Thank you so much for bringing her home, Annie. I appreciate it."

"No problem, Charlie Grace. Happy to do it." Annie turned her attention to Charlie Grace's father. "Missed you at church last Sunday, Clancy."

He huffed. "You think being in this wheelchair suddenly makes me a regular churchgoer?" Despite his gruff reply, there was a smile on his face.

"Well, we can only hope," came her teasing reply.

Annie and Pete Cumberland were some of her favorite people. They'd lived here in Thunder Mountain for as long as Charlie Grace could remember. Pete and Annie owned and ran the Rustic Pine Tavern, shelling out beer mugs on Saturday nights along with the best-grilled hamburgers this side of the Tetons. On Sunday mornings, Pete pastored a small congregation at Moose Chapel. Their black Lab, Bartender, was her daughter, Jewel's, favorite dog in the whole wide world—Jewel's words, not her own.

"So, when is the big opening?" Annie asked.

"Two weeks from yesterday," Charlie Grace told her. "I'm pretty nervous."

Her father gave another of his signature huffs.

"You should be proud of your daughter, Clancy. Not many women have what it takes to pivot in a whole new direction when needed."

"Well, not a whole new direction. The ranch operation will continue," Charlie Grace clarified.

"Just the same, it's a big thing. The whole town is proud of you." Annie checked her watch. "Well, I need to get."

"Thanks again for dropping off Jewel."

"My pleasure."

Charlie Grace walked Annie out to her car.

"So, how is Clancy?"

"Ornery as ever," Charlie Grace told her, kicking her stocking feet against the ground. "As you can tell, he's not happy with me right now."

Annie gave her a sympathetic look. "He'll come around. He loves you, you know."

She nodded. "Yeah, I do know."

"Don't try to do everything yourself. The good Lord never designed us with shoulders broad enough to carry it all without help. We're here...all of us."

Charlie Grace nodded. "Well, I am going to have to hire more ranch help." She told her about the unfortunate morning and how her new ranch hire failed to show up. "Know of anyone looking for work?"

Annie shook her head. "Not off hand. But I'll put the word out." She placed her palm on Charlie Grace's shoulder. "In the meantime, I can send Pete out if you need."

"What? In his spare time? Between the bar and the church, I think he has his work basket plenty full."

"He'd make time," Annie assured. "Funny how the Lord multiples our hours when we're willing to use them to serve others."

"Well, ask him to multiply a few of mine, would you?"

Annie laughed and climbed inside her truck. "I sure will."

Charlie Grace waved at Annie as she drove from the yard. She turned for the house and looked to the sky. "And multiply our bank account, too, while you're at it."

5

Reva wandered onto her deck wearing a plush robe tied at the waist and carrying a steaming cup of French press coffee. Just because she was in a remote area of Wyoming didn't mean she couldn't enjoy a flavorful brew.

The beans, sourced from a small roastery in the heart of Columbia, were expertly blended with spices from India and a touch of cocoa from Ghana. She had them shipped to her regularly despite the fact they often reminded her of Merritt Hardwick, the man she thought she was meant to spend her life with. Sadly, the relationship ended over seven years ago when she refused to move to Washington, D.C., and support his political aspirations.

Reva settled onto a cushioned deck chair and looked across the vista at the river below. This was her home. These mountains, these people. Thunder Mountain was where she belonged. Had she left with Merritt, she was convinced she might grow to hate him for enticing her to leave her heart behind.

Besides, she was needed here. The people of Thunder

Mountain weren't only clients and constituents; they were her friends. She supported them, and they had championed her in her worst struggles.

Still, she hadn't been prepared for the loneliness. Especially in the evenings when she and Merritt had often cuddled on the sofa and talked the nights away.

Reva unrolled the *Thunder Mountain Gazette* and laid it out on her lap. Her eyes scanned the headlines, stopping on a subject that was big news—the television production company that planted their outfit just outside Jackson and entirely too close for many locals liking.

The news piece was fair but held a definite slant toward protecting the area from the encroachment of outsiders...a term used multiple times by the paper's editor, Albie Baron.

She shut the paper and pushed it aside. To be expected, she supposed. The residents of Thunder Mountain had already seen a lot of change watching as nearby Jackson turned into a tourist hotspot. They did not easily embrace more, especially those individuals who believed the flood of tourism might creep into their tiny town.

Reva was about to wander back inside for a shower when her phone rang. It was Lila. "Hey, the farmer's market starts today. Want to go?"

"I thought you were working?"

"We were up all night with an emergency rectal prolapse repair. Doc Tillman told me to take the day off."

Reva grimaced. "Sounds painful."

"Yeah, just ask Frank Chapman's broodmare."

"I meant painful for you." Reva mentally checked her schedule for the day. "And, yes...I'd love to hit the farmer's market with you. I know Charlie Grace is up to her elbows with getting ready for the big opening day at Teton Trails, but do you want to invite Capri to meet us there?"

"Already did," came the reply.

The town held a farmer's market next to the high school football field every Tuesday and Saturday, weather permitting. Rows of tables perched underneath tent awnings displayed vibrant green kale, plump red tomatoes, and crispy cucumbers grown by locals and arranged neatly on display. The strawberries, raspberries, and piles of carrots, onions, and garlic bulbs were so fresh and fragrant that Reva could almost taste them just by standing there.

"Oh, my goodness. Look at those flowers!" Exclaimed Lila. "Nobody grows roses like Brittany Peters. She definitely has the magic touch."

Lila turned to Capri. "Speaking of that magic touch, how's your mom's garden coming along? I'm dying for some of her snap peas when they come on. They're great in a stir fry."

"Both she and her garden are fine," Capri told her. "And get this; Dick is out there helping her. My stepdad even bought her a new rototiller."

The news brought a smile to Reva's face. "That's good to hear." Dick hadn't always been supportive of his wife. But people can change, and Capri's stepfather was evidence of that fact.

Together, they wandered to a large booth filled with crocheted and knitted items for sale. There were baby booties, lap blankets, and even dog coats made with multi-colored yarn...all made with love by a group of ladies in town. Never ones to take themselves too seriously, these ladies called their little bunch the Knit Wits and donated sales proceeds to a benevolence fund maintained down at the bank to help neighbors in need.

Oma Griffith sat in a folding chair, fanning herself with a folded newspaper. "Well, hello girls."

"Hi, Oma." Reva gave the woman a little wave. She turned to Betty Dunning, who sat next to her. "Look at all this. You, ladies, have been busy." She pulled her wallet from her bag. "How's your arthritis, Betty?"

The older woman grinned and held out a purple-veined hand for inspection. "Oh, much better. I've been spending a lot of time with Ben—Bengay, that is," she let out a delighted squeal, pleased at her own joke.

Reva, Lila, and Capri laughed with her. Her jokes were much easier to stomach than her often over-described tales of sicknesses either she or her friends had endured. No ailment was off limits, even those that included bodily fluids. She was one of those people who spent hours on social media posting and commenting on graphic photos of infected and oozing toes and the like. Betty Dunning was fascinated with medical issues and could offer up a remedy for everything. If you could recite the symptoms, she had the cure.

"Well, Betty. Looks like Bengay is a keeper." She turned to Oma. "How much?" Reva asked, holding up her wallet.

Oma put her knitting needles aside. "Which item, dear?"

"I want it all," Reva told them. "Pack it all up and have the items delivered to the nursing home. Well, except for those baby booties. I guess I'll take them."

Oma and Betty's eyes widened. "You sure?" Oma asked. "The total comes to a pretty penny," she warned.

Reva handed them a wad of hundred-dollar bills. "That should cover it."

Before they could thank her and get the booties bagged up, a loud voice shouted from behind them. "Help!"

Reva turned toward the commotion. A man she didn't recognize gripped his throat and doubled over, gasping for air. Panicked, he folded to his knees in front of the cupcake booth and waved his arm frantically in the air for help.

Reva quickly grabbed Lila's hand and pulled her in that direction. "Let's go!" Capri followed close behind.

The woman at the booth who had shouted for help looked

frantic. "He's choking," she explained, pointing to a cupcake decorated with a tiny jellybean on top of a mound of frosting.

Before Reva could move into action, she felt a push that nearly knocked her off her feet. She was shoved aside by a forceful Betty Dunning, who had raced to join them. The petite white-haired woman planted her feet about a foot apart, squared her small frame, and wrapped her arms tightly around the man's waist. "One, two, three..." She squeezed with a quick upward thrust. Without waiting for a reaction, she repeated the procedure—harder this time.

That did the trick. The man coughed, and a tiny red jellybean flew out of his mouth and landed on the grass at his feet. His purple-hued facial skin immediately brightened and returned to its natural pink tone.

The crowd that had assembled let out a collective sigh of relief as the man regained his composure and nodded his head. "I'm good. I'm okay."

When he'd collected himself a bit more, he turned and gave Betty a bear hug. "Thank you! You saved my life!"

Betty's cheeks blushed pink. "It was nothing." She patted his back. "Glad to be of help."

As the commotion died down, they all turned and walked back to Oma and Betty's booth. Reva shook her head. "Wow, Betty. You acted fast. How did you know what to do?"

Betty grinned back at her. "YouTube."

6

A fter a late night holed up in her home office poring over the financial projections she'd prepared for the bank, Charlie Grace had fallen into bed and woken up exhausted.

Reva warned her to keep the numbers realistic—and she had—even so, the figures staring back at her were daunting. There were so many factors out of her control.

Would anyone actually show up and lay out cash to stay here? Especially when there were other guest ranches in the area that were established and doing well.

Would her new website entice vacationers to spend their vacations in those newly built guest cabins? Despite her best plans, could she offer the kind of rustic vacations and opportunity to connect with nature that executives, their spouses, and children couldn't get in the city? Word of mouth was essential in the hospitality industry. She'd need her guests to return home happy and willing to tell friends about the wonderful time they'd had in the mountains of Wyoming while staying at Teton Trails.

The idea of it all left her head spinning.

Charlie Grace shook off her worries and got dressed. There was no sense in pondering something she had no way of knowing. She'd done her best to prepare for the opening this weekend. Now, she could only wait and see if her effort had been worth it.

"Where are you going?" her dad asked as she pulled her farm jacket from the hook by the back door.

"Out to feed and then to town."

"I suppose you think you can keep up with this ranching operation while catering to all those city folks wanting their beds turned down at night." He wheeled over to the table and pulled the top off the sugar bowl. "Don't think I don't know what time you went to bed last night. You might think you're some superwoman, but you're just regular folks, like the rest of us." He scooped a heaping spoonful of sugar into his coffee mug and stirred. "Something's going to give, Charlie Grace. This ranch will suffer."

The muscles in her neck tightened. "I'm good, Dad. Besides, after I get done feeding, I'm heading to town. I plan to stop at the newspaper office and place an ad in the *Thunder Mountain Gazette* for Roy Mullin's replacement." She'd learned that most ranch hands didn't frequent the internet want ads. "I'll get someone hired for the feeding. Until then, I can handle it."

Her father huffed. "So, you think you've got it all under control?"

Feeling annoyed, she nodded. "I do. By this time next week, those two cowboys I hired from Dubois will be here to help with the guest ranch."

"Suit yourself, sister," he said, pulling the mug to his lips. "But those guys you hired are old. They're anything but ranch hands. Bet they're too feeble to lift fifty pounds, let alone ride a horse for more than two hours at a time."

She pulled her coat on without telling him that Whit Hawthorne and Merritt Tilman were all she could afford right now. "They're not so old they can't lead some trail rides, cook outdoor barbecue, and sit around a campfire playing their guitars. Trust me, Dad, we're good."

Charlie Grace hurried out the door to avoid further judgment.

The internet called her hometown one of the last real old-west towns in America. With a population of nine hundred seventy-two, Thunder Mountain was noted to be a hidden gem with the authentic feel of the frontier set against the scenic backdrop of the majestic peaks of the Tetons.

She didn't know about all that. What she did know was that the small town was indeed quaint and filled with history. Many buildings along Main Street were built over a hundred years ago.

Heading into Thunder Mountain from the main highway, you passed the school—circa the 1960s—and the same school she had attended. The most prominent building housed the high school classes, the gymnasium, and the science lab. The grade school and junior high were in the smaller building. A shop and the ball fields were beyond that.

Next was the Western Drug and Grocery. The proximity to the school was handy for students who trekked the short walk to purchase bags of Doritos and cherry colas on their lunch break. Personally, Charlie Grace had always taken advantage of every opportunity to eat hot lunch. Mrs. Rudd's homemade pizza was piled high with real cheese, fried hamburger meat, and sliced black olives. Her mouth watered, simply remembering how good it tasted. Never mind that the dessert served often included massive chocolate chip oatmeal cookies, fresh from the oven.

Who would trade that for a bag of Doritos?

The center of town held a cluster of rustic establishments lined with wooden boardwalks. Yellow rosebushes tumbled blooms over the occasional fence line, and most doorways were semi-blocked with a sleeping dog. There was the Rustic Pine Tavern and Grill, Bear Country Gifts, Bluebird Books, and Thunder Mountain Bank and Trust. At the far end of Main Street, on the right, was the town hall and then her destination —the *Thunder Mountain Gazette.*

Charlie Grace eased her truck into the angled parking spot in front and cut her motor. She grabbed her bag and climbed out.

"Hey, Charlie Grace!"

She looked in the direction of the voice and noted that her boyfriend's mother was heading her way. "Hi, Oma." She waved.

"Oh, honey. I'm so glad I ran into you today. I was talking to Jason at dinner last night, and he says the guest ranch is opening this weekend." She clasped her hands together with excitement.

Charlie Grace nodded. "That's right."

"Are you nervous? My boy tells me you're a little worried no one will show up."

Charlie Grace held back a sigh, unsure how she felt about her discussions with Jason being shared with his mother. She made a mental note to mention the matter to him.

Not that she believed Oma held any ill will. The entire town adored Oma Griffith, a widow who was known for being compassionate and generous, often delivering meals to anyone who fell ill. Kids in town had spent hours in her home after school, playing card games.

Once, Charlie Grace went to the cemetery to put flowers on her mother's grave and found Oma sitting in a lawn chair next to where her beloved Earl was buried. "You know, the sky looks a lot different when you have someone up there," was all Oma said.

Remembering this, Charlie Grace felt nothing but compassion for the woman before her. She pulled her phone from her purse. "Would you like to see the new sign out at the ranch?" She poised the phone so that Oma could get a good look at the images.

"Oh, Charlie Grace. It's becoming so real. I am so proud of you."

Oma would make a lovely mother-in-law. Even so, Charlie Grace knew she would never marry her son for more reasons than she had time to go into. Right now, she had to place an ad for some ranch help.

She drew Oma into a hug. "Thank you. That means so much." She straightened and pointed toward the door leading to the news office. "Look, I wish I had more time to chat, but...."

Oma waved her hand. "Go. You have a lot to do, no doubt."

Charlie Grace bid her goodbye and turned for the newspaper office entrance, flanked by half-barrel planters packed full of pink petunias, daisies, and blue lobelia flowing over the sides. She opened the door, and a little bell tinkled.

"Hello," she called out into the empty room.

Albie Barton peeked his head from the back room. His tie hung loose against his white button-down shirt, rolled at the sleeves. Cobwebs were hanging from his ruffled dark hair. "Oh, sorry. I was in the attic space looking for some old issues."

"Old issues?"

"Yeah, I thought of resurrecting an article about America's bicentennial. I must've mismarked those boxes. There wasn't a thing in the one labeled 1976."

"Sorry." It was all Charlie Grace could think of to say.

Albie brushed the palms of his hands together. "Well, enough of that. What can I do you for?"

Charlie Grace grabbed her wallet. "I need to place an ad in the classified section. For a ranch hand," she added.

"You bet. Let's get you taken care of."

The bell rang, pulling both of their attention toward the door. In walked Nicola Cavendish, known for her love of martinis...and gossip. "Well, hello, you two." The words poured from her lips like syrup as she directed her gaze at Charlie Grace. "Did I overhear you're placing an ad for a ranch hand?"

Charlie Grace nodded, hating to confirm her business with the banker's wife, who was known for sharing information liberally around town.

"Well, isn't that interesting?"

Charlie Grace frowned. "Interesting? Why?"

Nicola's mouth drew into a slow, wide grin. "Because I just saw your ex-husband coming out of the Rustic Pine. He said he'd just been hired by your dad."

7

Charlie Grace pressed her foot on the brake so hard the tires threw gravel. She jumped from the pickup and headed for the house, taking the porch steps two at a time.

The wise thing might be to stop and take a deep breath—right here and right now. Charlie Grace threw wisdom to the wind and opened the door with the same force that had slammed into her when she heard Nicola Cavendish's announcement.

"Dad!" she shouted. She glanced around the empty living room and headed for the hallway leading to his bedroom. "Dad," she repeated, louder this time.

His door opened. "What's all the shouting about?"

She jabbed her finger in his direction, madder than she'd ever been at him. "You know good and well why I'm fired up! You hired Gibbs? Are you out of your mind?"

His face remained unmoved. "Settle down. And don't forget whom you're talking to. You may be over thirty, but I'm still your father." He lifted his chin slightly. "You may not acknowledge your limits, but anyone with a mind can see you are working yourself to death. Add that cockamamie guest ranch idea, and you're—" He stopped midsentence and quickly wheeled over to the large picture window overlooking the Teton range.

He pointed. "See those jagged mountains?"

Charlie Grace folded her arms across her chest and remained silent.

"Well, sister—those peaks were formed from rockslides. Rockslides that occurred when the underlying earth could no longer take the pressure of the ice that had formed and was beginning to melt. The understructure simply gave way... changed the whole damn landscape, often taking trees and a few animals with it."

He wheeled to face her and locked his gaze with her own. "You are setting Teton Trails up for the same. Worse? You could go down with it. Last night wasn't the first all-nighter in your office. You may claim you have everything handled, but I see the worry etched on your face."

"What, pray tell, does that have to do with hiring my ex-husband? Do you think having him around here every day is going to help? And, just so you know, I was in town placing an ad for a ranch hand. I told you that."

This time her father remained silent. When he finally spoke, his voice was firm. "Gibbs Nichols knows this ranch. I trust him like a son. He's a good man."

"A good man who engaged in extracurricular activities with multiple women in this town and beyond." She lifted her left hand. "There's a good reason there's no longer a ring on that finger."

If that man in the wheelchair dared to roll his eyes like he had on so many prior occasions when the subject of her divorce came up, she swore she would march over and punch him... invalid or not.

He opened his mouth. "Charlie Grace, we're talking business. You need to take the emotion out of this."

She clenched her fists, restraining her earlier thought of pummeling him. "You want me to put my emotions in the cupboard and slam the door shut, just like Mom did? Well, I'm not Mom. And Gibbs is not working here!"

The back door opened, and Gibbs strode in with Jewel. He wore tight jeans, a leather jacket, and had his aviator sunglasses tucked on top of his highly moussed reddish-brown hair like some celebrity. "Hey, did I just hear my name?"

Before she could open her mouth to respond, Jewel pulled her hand from his and ran for Charlie Grace. "Mom? Did you hear the good news? Daddy is going to work here at the ranch again. We'll get to see him every day. Every—single—day. Not just when it's my turn at his house." She quickly looked between the two of them, beaming. "God answered my prayers."

Charlie Grace groaned inside. She could barely breathe, immediately recognizing defeat.

She bit at the inside of her cheek for a moment, then huffed. "Okay...okay! But this is only temporary." She looked at Gibbs, then back at her dad. "And I mean it."

8

C harlie Grace checked her phone for the time as she walked towards the Rustic Pine. It was Friday evening, and despite all that she had on her shoulders right now, she was anxious to set it all aside for a few hours and focus on something else. Maybe even have some fun.

Luke Cunningham, her former high school friend, tipped his cowboy hat and smiled as they passed on the sidewalk.

"Hey, Luke," she said. "How's life treating you?"

He responded with a grin. "Better than a lick and a promise." His smile widened, deepening his dimples. "You?"

She assured him she was doing fine, as well.

He granted her a pleased nod. "Well, you take care." He headed down the boardwalk whistling.

Charlie Grace pushed open the door to the bar and was immediately greeted with the familiar scent of wood smoke and grilling hamburgers. The bar was dimly lit and crowded. She looked around, scanning the room for her friends. It didn't take long to spot them waving at her from their corner table.

"Hey, Charlie Grace!" Capri greeted as she approached.

"Well, you look downright stressed," Lila noted as she brought a long-neck beer bottle to her lips.

Charlie Grace slid into the waiting empty chair. "I have no business being here, not when Teton Trails opens in less than two days." She placed her purse at her feet under the varnished wooden table. "Have you guys been waiting long?"

"Depends on how you define long?" Reva smiled as she pointed to her watch.

Charlie Grace took in the familiar surroundings, walls adorned with western-themed paintings and photographs of cowboys and horses. A Garth Brooks song played from the old-fashioned jukebox against the wall.

"I'm sorry I'm late," she explained. "Couldn't be helped. The water pump was acting up in the pickup. I had to replace it." She waved at Annie, who gave her a nod and headed her way from behind the bar.

"You replaced the water pump?" Lila looked at her incredulously. She leaned over and wiped a smear from Charlie Grace's chin. "You never cease to amaze me."

Charlie Grace shrugged. "It's not hard. The difficult part is getting the timing belt back in and working right."

Charlie Grace and her girlfriends met as often as they could —sometimes for breakfast, and nearly every Friday night for food, drinks, and conversation. At times, they gathered at one of their houses. Most often, they met here at the Rustic Pine. They even had their own table tucked in the corner, facilitated by Annie, who had an intentional habit of saving it by leaving the surface uncleared until the first of them arrived.

The Rustic Pine was not known as the rowdy bar in town. That would be Moosehead Tavern, where whiskey flowed freely and fights often broke out, prompting a visit from Fleet Southcott. Ignoring city code, Fleet rarely planted any of the offenders in jail. Instead, he took them home and tucked the culprits onto their sofas with blankets, warning them to sober up before returning to town for their vehicles.

"Here you go, honey." Annie planted a margarita on the table in front of Charlie Grace. "Just the way you like it...with extra salt on the rim and next to no alcohol."

Charlie Grace smiled at her. "Thanks, Annie. How's Pete tonight?"

Annie nodded in the direction of the bar. "Like every Friday night...busy." She patted Reva's shoulder, then returned to the bar with their black Lab, Bartender, following at her feet.

"Busy is right." Lila looked around. "There are a lot of people in here I don't recognize."

Reva leaned across the table and spoke just loud enough for them to hear over the music. "I have a feeling many of them are with that production company."

Capri nodded. "Yeah, I hear they start filming in a couple of weeks."

Reva jiggled the ice in her glass of Diet Coke. "My office has been clamoring with people dropping by to voice their concerns."

"Concerns?" Charlie Grace asked.

"Most of it is just being nosy. Apparently, Nicola Cavendish read in the entertainment papers that the television series is expected to create a housing boom here in the area. She felt it her duty to spread that tidbit and elevate worry, of course."

"Worry?" Capri twisted the cap off her beer bottle. "Seems to me an influx of tourists is a good thing...at least for Grand Teton Water Adventures. Vacationers love to take whitewater rafting trips."

"Maybe so," Reva agreed. "But the housing thing indicates that the show might glamorize our neck of the woods and encourage people looking to escape more urban areas to move here. That will result in raised prices and soaring taxes. No one wants Thunder Mountain to become another Jackson."

"Move here for good?" Lila asked. She waved at Oma Griffith and her Knit Wit friends, who sat with their yarn at a table across the room. "Do they know we don't have a Costco for hundreds of miles?"

"Well, I've got much bigger things to worry about," Charlie Grace announced. "Dad hired Gibbs."

Lila's eyes went big. "What?"

Capri added her surprise. "He hired your ex-husband?"

Charlie Grace took a sip of her margarita. "Yup. Dad seems to think I can't juggle everything right now, and we all know he thinks Gibbs walks on water."

Reva shook her head in disbelief. "Oh, Gibbs should have had the good sense to turn down that offer. What was he thinking?"

"He wasn't," Charlie Grace said. "But then, why should he start using good judgment now?"

All of them nodded in solidarity. It was no secret that Gibbs had put Charlie Grace through her own personal hell regarding her marriage. Her girlfriends had been in the arena with her through it all. They liked Gibbs—he was a likable guy—but they all knew he could also be a weasel and wanted firm boundaries when it came to his access to their good friend.

"And you said yes to this?" Capri asked her.

"I didn't have a choice. Not when he used our daughter as a prod in the situation."

"Ouch!" Capri said.

"Yeah, apparently, she's been praying for her daddy to move back home so he can be with her every day. I mean, what was I supposed to say to that?" She took another gulp from her margarita, already feeling the faint alcohol. She'd always been a lightweight when it came to drinking, which is why she was so careful. She didn't like feeling out of control.

Reva covered her hand with her own. "Girl, sounds like you were placed in a bad situation all around. You did the right thing under the circumstances. Besides, you're the boss. He answers to you now. While your father may have hired him, you have the power to fire him. Don't let him forget it."

Charlie Grace lifted her chin slightly. "That's right. Gibbs Nichols had better toe the line, or else." She waved off the subject. "Enough about me. What about you guys? We didn't get much of a chance to talk out at the gate the other day. Catch me up."

Capri slid her chair back and stood.

"Where are you going?" Reva asked.

"Annie's swamped. I'm going to go get us another round." When the girls all went for their purses, she shook her head. "This one's on me."

Charlie Grace watched her friend weave through the crowd. "What about you, Lila? How's vet school going?"

Her pretty dark-haired friend rolled her blue eyes and sighed. "It's much harder than I thought it would be. We had a visiting prof from UC Davis here this week."

Lila had already obtained her DVM designation. Based on dozens of recommendations, she'd landed a coveted spot in UC Davis's large animal veterinary extension program. The extra classes while interning for Doc Tillman had her burning candles at both ends.

"Oh? Tell us more," Reva urged.

Lila fidgeted with her beer bottle. "His presentation was on the nonsurgical obstetric management of dystocia. While a transverse presentation is very rare in cattle, the condition is found more often in horses ending in lost foals." She shuddered. "Next week, I have a clinical where I will practice repulsion and rotation. They bring in a life-sized dummy horse."

Charlie Grace grimaced. "Sounds painful...even if the horse is made of plastic."

"Don't I know? Camille was born breech. Remember?"

Reva nodded. "How can we forget? We were so worried that night."

Capri showed back up at the table with a tray filled with bottles and glasses. "Worried about what?" she asked as she distributed the drinks.

Reva reached for her glass and slipped her empty onto Capri's waiting tray. "We were remembering the night Camille was born."

Lila laughed. "I thought that nothing could be harder than a scary birth. It turns out I was wrong. Having a teenage daughter in the house is a lot like running a blender without a top on it."

Charlie Grace quickly empathized. "And no one is more passionate about their child-rearing opinions than women who don't have kids."

Reva frowned. "Hey, now."

Charlie Grace playfully punched her girlfriend's upper arm. "Not you. I was talking about...." She let her voice drift and nodded toward Nicola Cavendish, who had just entered the bar and was heading for Oma's table with her knitting bag in hand. "I'm not trying to talk trash, but when Nicola wears her hair up like that, doesn't she look a lot like Mrs. Oleson in *Little House on the Prairie*?"

"Mrs. Oleson didn't wear jeans." Capri fixed her gaze on the woman's boots. "And custom Lucchese's."

Reva turned. "Oh, my goodness. Those are gorgeous."

"Down, girl. You already own at least six pairs," Charlie Grace reminded.

Reva frowned. "Not every aspect of life needs to be approached with caution. I was being spontaneous when I bought each and every pair of those boots. You know what that word means, right?"

Lila laughed. "Are you speaking to Charlie Grace?"

"I'm spontaneous," Charlie Grace argued, then added

tongue-in-cheek, "Just because I'm a divorced mom who runs a ranch and works from morning until night doesn't mean I don't know how to have spur-of-the-moment fun."

They all nodded. "Right."

Capri gathered the remaining empty bottles and put them on the tray. "Speaking of fun, how's Jason Griffith these days?"

Charlie Grace's shoulders stiffened. "He's just fine. Why?"

Reva's eyes sparkled with amusement. "The man celebrated your one-year dating anniversary by giving you a box set of flavored mustards."

Charlie Grace was quick to defend him. "He ordered them online from Poland. He says their popular Kamis Stołowa is extraordinarily flavorful, a Dijon highly reminiscent of horse radish."

Capri hoisted the tray onto her shoulder. "No offense, Charlie Grace, but a truckload of spicy mustard won't erase the fact that the guy you're dating is bland." She tilted her head in the direction of the bar. "Unlike that guy. Man, he's hot. I mean, he looks just like McDreamy from *Grey's Anatomy*."

They all turned to check the guy out.

Charlie Grace felt a quick intake of breath. She wasn't a guy ogler, but Capri was right. This guy was very good-looking. He wore a brown leather jacket that matched the bourbon-amber color of his hair. As if on cue, he turned, and they locked gazes.

Her heartbeat quickened.

Even from here, she could see his chiseled jawline and athletic build. His body language was confident—the epitome of an attractive and charming man who undoubtedly left a lasting impression on anyone who crossed his path.

His near-perfect face broke into a warm, inviting smile.

Maybe it was the tequila, but she felt flushed and quickly looked away without returning the gesture.

Reva noticed. "What's all that about? Why'd you do that?"

"Do what?"

Reva rolled her eyes.

Charlie Grace grunted. "Unlike Capri, I'm not into heartthrobs."

Capri shrugged. "Suit yourself," she teased before carrying the tray back to the bar.

Reva leaned close. "The bigger question is why are you dating someone who is about as much fun as the legal doctrines of desuetude."

Charlie Grace ignored her friend's barb and lifted her second margarita to her lips. She took a long swig and winced. "Who made this? It's strong."

Lila pointed. "Pete made it. He might not have known it was for you."

For a second, Charlie Grace considered returning the cocktail and asking for a lighter version. She quickly dismissed the idea. The last thing she wanted was to act like a Karen and make a fuss. She'd simply have to drink slower.

As the night wore on, the bar filled with more patrons. The music got louder, and the conversations became more boisterous. Lila ordered another round of drinks.

Charlie Grace was surprised to find her glass empty. She held up her hand. "Not for me."

Capri gave her a stern look. "Oh, come on. Live a little. Have some of that spur-of-the-moment fun you talk about."

"No, really. I already feel that last one."

Lila wasn't buying it. "Look, none of us wants you inebriated. But the first barely had any tequila, so technically, this will only be your second."

Charlie Grace hesitated, then shrugged. "Okay, maybe one more. But make this one a root beer."

Reva laughed while Capri and Lila groaned in unison. "You're hopeless, you know that?" Capri teased.

When the drinks arrived, Capri unscrewed the top on her

own beer. Suddenly, she stood and announced, "I'm going to dance."

The others looked at her incredulously. "Dance?" Lila asked, raising her eyebrows.

Capri grinned. "Yes, dance! Come on, girls. Let's have some fun!"

Charlie Grace and Reva exchanged an amused look, then stood and followed Capri onto the dance floor, where a few couples were already swaying to the music. Laughing, Charlie Grace, Lila, and Reva joined in.

Charlie Grace felt the stress of the week melting away as she let herself get lost in the fun.

As the night wore on, they danced and drank and laughed, leaving Charlie Grace feeling like a carefree student once again. Finally, the bar began to empty out, and they decided it was time to call it a night.

As they walked out of the Rustic Pine, arms looped together, the chilly night air hit them.

Charlie Grace looked across the street and saw that guy—the one who had been sitting at the bar. He stood with his hands in his jean pockets, watching them.

Their gazes locked again, and he smiled in her direction.

This time she smiled back.

9

R eva climbed from her Cadillac Escalade, taking care not to let the heels of her Gianvito Rossi pumps dig into the dirt in the church parking lot. Some would say wearing stilettos anywhere but on a paved sidewalk was asking for trouble, and they'd be right. They'd also be right to claim her elaborate wide-brimmed straw hat was out of place in the wilds of Wyoming.

Her extended family was from the South. She'd spent a lot of time with them while growing up, and especially during the time she attended Tulane. In the words of her dearly departed Memaw, "No respectable black woman spends time in Jesus' house with her head uncovered."

Capri exited her car and waved. "Hey, Reva. Morning!" She opened the back passenger door and helped her mom and stepdad from the back seat. "Save us a seat."

Reva nodded and joined the small crowd making their way up the steps and into the tiny log church. Moose Chapel was constructed in 1925, which predated the establishment of Grand Teton National Park. Located fifteen miles south of town, the tiny log building with the rustic cross on top was a beacon to everyone, but not only on Sundays. The doors were always open to anyone needing to pray and have time for reflection.

It was not uncommon for Pastor Pete to stand behind the pulpit on Sunday mornings, counseling that the congregants were the true ambassadors of the Lord. He backed up his claim by quoting his favorite scripture, "You are a living epistle, written not of ink but of the spirit of God." While no one counted, Pete had wooed more souls at the Rustic Pine than in this church building.

Reva made her way down the wood-slatted aisle to her spot on a pew next to Charlie Grace, Lila, and their families. Capri and her parents followed close behind.

Reva looked around. "Some folks are missing this morning."

Capri took her seat nearby and pulled a hymnal from the rack on the pew in front of her. She leaned and answered with a low voice. "I heard a new Baptist church opened in Jackson. Nicola was overheard telling a group in the post office that she was gathering some folks to check it out."

Reva felt her eyebrows raise. "Is that so?" While she applauded a new church, she couldn't imagine worshipping anywhere but Moose Chapel.

She waved to Annie perched at the piano with her fingers poised on the keys. The congregation stood and sang several of Reva's personal favorites, ending with "In the Garden," a hymn she'd sung as a child.

Annie closed the wooden lid on the piano keys, signaling they should take their seats and turn their attention to the sermon.

Pastor Pete brought his A-game this Sunday and preached a powerful message that left the attendees filing out of the church with wide smiles. "I don't know how that guy does it, but he always leaves me feeling the need to be better...to do better," Charlie Grace commented as she took her daughter's hand and led her down the front steps.

Capri pulled her phone from her bag and turned the volume back on. "Careful, if you get any more benevolent, we'll be calling you Saint Charlie Grace."

Charlie Grace waved off her comment. "Whatever!"

Lila smoothed some wrinkles from her dress. "You guys have time to catch lunch?"

"Not today," Charlie Grace answered. "I've got to get back to the ranch. Our first guests arrive tomorrow!"

They all shared in her enthusiasm by hugging her. "It's a dream come true."

"I don't know about that. If this new endeavor pays the bills, I'll be good."

Capri turned to the other two. "What about you guys? You up for some lunch in town?"

Lila shook her head. "I can't. I'm studying this afternoon."

Reva begged off as well. "I have a meeting in a few minutes. Why don't you take your mom? I'll give Dick a ride home after the meeting."

Capri slowly nodded. "Okay, then. Thanks." They hugged briefly.

Reva turned to Capri's stepdad. "You ready?"

He nodded, and she linked arms and led him back inside.

The basement was lined with folding chairs. Against the back wall stood a long table covered with a disposable paper tablecloth topped with a large box filled with donuts and maple bars on one end. On the other end, paper coffee cups and a basket filled with packets of sugar and creamer were neatly arranged next to a stainless-steel coffee urn.

Dick immediately scanned the donut box and lifted a chocolate-covered one onto a napkin. He turned. "Can I get you a maple bar, Reva?"

She smiled back at him. "No thanks, Dick." She pointed to her hips. "Watching my figure."

That brought a smile to his face. "Me, too." He followed up the statement with a big bite of the donut.

Reva made her way past a row of empty chairs and sat next to Dorothy Montgomery. "Hey, Dorothy." The middle-aged woman's hands shook. "You okay, Dot?"

"Yeah," was her response. Though her face didn't seem to agree.

Reva reached for her hand and gave a silent squeeze.

Minutes later, the meeting began. Reva grabbed her well-worn and dog-eared copy of the Big Book and headed for the podium. "Hey, everyone...let's take our seats."

The tiny group of folks at the back found their chairs and bowed their heads.

Reva cleared her throat. "God grant us the serenity to accept the things we cannot change, courage to change the things we can, and the wisdom to know the difference. Amen."

She raised her head and looked out over the familiar faces, the ones who gathered with her here every week. "Hi, my name is Reva Nygard. I'm an alcoholic."

10

Charlie Grace stared at the ceiling in her dark bedroom, wide awake hours before the alarm was scheduled to go off.

Today was the big day...the opening of Teton Trails Guest Ranch. According to her new reservation software, three guests were scheduled to arrive this morning. A family of four from Utah, an older couple from Florida, and a man, who had listed his address as a post office box in California, would be checking in and joining them for dinner.

She'd spent most of yesterday thinking and rethinking her plans. Word of mouth was everything to a start-up hospitality business. She needed these early ranch guests to leave happy. So happy, they would not only return but would tell all their friends about their wonderful time at Teton Trails.

Charlie Grace pushed back the handmade quilt her mother had made and climbed from the warm sheets. She flicked on the bedside lamp and headed for her office to work on the social media ads she'd tackled yesterday. No sense in wasting time.

Charlie Grace knew the cost of vacationing here at the

ranch was not cheap. Her new website promised "an authentic western experience" and included accommodations in one of the newly built log cabins, homemade meals in the main lodge, authentic western barbecues around a campfire, and plenty of outdoor activities.

She'd hired Aunt Mo to lead the kitchen staff—well, the staff they'd eventually hire as they grew big enough to warrant additional help. Until then, it was just her and Aunt Mo. The operating loan Reva had helped her secure from the bank would make payments on the van she'd purchased to transport guests to and from the Jackson Hole airport when needed. She'd also now have funds to contract with Capri for white-water excursions and to pay Ford Keaton for outdoor chuck-wagon meals. No matter his older age, Ford was known as the best barbecue chef around. His charbroiled steaks cooked over an open fire could bring a man to his knees.

If things went as she hoped over these early weeks, there would be an income stream that would allow her to pay Whit Hawthorne and Merritt Tillman for extra trail rides, guided fly-fishing, and high mountain lake hikes. Until that time, she was going to have to wear a lot of hats.

She was up for it.

By the time she closed her laptop and headed for the shower, she already had a long mental list of tasks to be accomplished before the guests arrived.

When she'd dressed and made her bed, Charlie Grace headed down the hallway, stopping for a moment at her daughter's room. Jewel was still sound asleep. She pulled her phone out and sent herself a text, a reminder that her daughter would need lunch money.

By the time she stepped onto the front porch, the sun began to peek over the jagged peaks of the Teton mountains in the distance. The stunning site caused her to pause and draw a deep breath, taking in the crisp morning air.

As she looked over the sprawling property, she couldn't help but feel a sense of pride and accomplishment. Running a ranch was no easy feat, but she'd always been drawn to hard work and the freedom of this lifestyle. She'd spent years working alongside her father. Since his accident, everything had fallen on her shoulders.

But today was no day for resting on her laurels. Charlie Grace had a full day ahead of her. She checked her watch and headed across the grass lawn, past the guest cabins, and in the direction of the main lodge, built of raw logs with a sprawling wraparound porch sporting rocking chairs and tables with newly purchased chess boards and decks of cards in baskets on the floor.

The two-story lodge had been built by her grandfather years before to house cowboys and ranch workers. The upstairs was lined with a hallway with doors leading to individual rooms. It was on Charlie Grace's agenda to eventually remodel those rooms with attached private bathrooms. Right now, her budget forced her to delay that phase. Currently, all she could afford was some sprucing up of the downstairs, adding leather sofas and new rugs along with some special paintings from a local artist. The kitchen remained unaltered and would be off-limits to guests.

In the far distance were the barns and corrals, also built by her grandfather. When he'd taken over, her father had constructed a loading chute and a machinery shed that housed the trucks and equipment. He'd also built their massive horse barn with individual stalls and a tackle room. The barn was painted white and was emblazoned with their ranch logo.

Charlie Grace climbed the steps to the wooden porch and headed inside the lodge. The smell of coffee and sizzling bacon immediately hit her nose. She followed the aroma to the kitchen, where she found Aunt Mo standing at the stove. "You're preparing breakfast?" she asked, puzzled.

"Honey, didn't you see my note?"

"What note?"

"The one I left on the kitchen counter." Her aunt wiped her hands on a towel tucked inside the band of her apron. "That family is coming in early. They called and said they'd be here this morning. Asked what time we served breakfast." She pulled a carton of eggs from the refrigerator. "Of course, I said we'd have a meal ready when they arrived." She glanced at the wall clock. "Which should be soon."

Aunt Mo pointed to a bowl just out of her reach. Charlie Grace handed it to her. "I hope that's okay. I figured it's what you'd want." She set to cracking eggs into the bowl. "I tried to call you on your cell, but you didn't pick up. By the way, your voicemail box is full."

Charlie Grace frowned and pulled her phone from her jeans pocket, confirming that what her aunt said was true. "Sorry," she shrugged. "I'll go through and clean the messages up later."

She grabbed an apron and tied it on. "Now, what do you need help with?"

Aunt Mo gave her a rundown of all that had to be done. Together they worked to prepare a baked egg casserole to go with the fried bacon and hash browns with homemade biscuits.

"Mmm...something smells good."

Charlie Grace looked up to see Gibbs in the doorway. "Now, why is it that you always show up when there's bacon frying?" she asked, pouring herself a second mug of coffee.

"Well, good morning to you, too," he said, helping himself to a crisp slice from the plate Aunt Mo held in her hand.

The older woman smiled and handed him another.

Charlie Grace wasn't as generous. "If you start eating breakfast here, the cost will be deducted from your wages," she warned. "Besides, you have a lot to do. Shouldn't you be out at the barns doing it?"

He moved to slap her on the butt. "Oh, settle down."

She caught his hand before it hit its mark. "I mean it, Gibbs. This job ain't no free ride."

He lifted the mug from her hand and took a sip. "Like I said, no reason to fret. The feedings are all done. You're getting low on grain, though, so I plan to head in and grab some sacks from Wylie's." He pulled a crumpled piece of paper and a pen from his back pants pocket. "You need anything else while I'm in town?"

She shook her head, choosing not to acknowledge his completed chores. "Don't go dawdling in town. You're on my time clock, and I'm not paying you to chat up the boys at the Feed and Seed." Despite the weak smile on her face, she gave him a look that meant business.

Gibbs responded with a tip of his hat and a wide grin. "Yes, boss."

As soon as the door shut behind him, Charlie Grace turned to Aunt Mo and groaned out loud.

"Oh, honey. It would be best if you quit letting Gibbs get under your skin like that. Robs you of peace."

"You're right." Charlie Grace moved for the sink and tossed the remains of her coffee down the drain. "Right now, I've got to get a little girl up and ready for school. Should only take me a few minutes, and then I'll get back over here."

Aunt Mo placed the platter of bacon into the oven next to the egg casserole to stay warm. "Well, honey. You best let me do that. It looks like your first guests have arrived." She pointed out the window.

An SUV wound its way up the lane.

The palms on Charlie Grace's hands suddenly turned clammy. All the dreaming, the planning, the preparation—now it was show time.

Her aunt seemed to sense what she was feeling. "It's the dawning of a new day here at Teton Trails." She squeezed Charlie Grace's hands in her own. "Savor this moment. You've worked hard, Charlie Grace."

She couldn't help it. Her eyelids burned with unshed tears. She blinked away the emotion. "Yup...a new day."

She smiled at her aunt and then headed out the door to greet her first guests.

11

C harlie Grace found herself strangely excited as she headed across the front porch and watched the SUV doors open. Out climbed a man who looked to be in his forties wearing chinos, a polo shirt, and loafers. The woman, who she guessed must be his wife, had long brown hair pulled back into a ponytail. She wore a floral T-shirt dress and stylish canvas sports shoes in a shade of pink that matched the pattern in her dress. Two adorable children exited the back passenger seat—a boy and a girl who looked very near the same age.

"Wow!" said the boy, looking all around.

"There's horses!" The girl pointed toward the corrals. "Real ones."

That brought a smile to Charlie Grace's face. "Welcome. You must be the Clark family," she said, moving down the stairs with an outstretched hand. "I'm Charlie Grace Rivers, one of the owners here at Teton Trails."

She helped them unload their luggage and learned that Jay and Gail Clark were from Logan, Utah. Jay was a software engineer, and his wife was a stay-at-home mom who homeschooled their twin children, age nine. Kyle and Kaylie.

"Let's get you settled," Charlie Grace suggested. She led them to the biggest guest cabin, a two-room log structure with a fireplace and a kitchenette. "You have a coffee pot and sodas in the refrigerator, all complimentary." She turned to the kids. "The snacks in the basket are also for you."

Kyle's eyes widened. "Yum! I love candy bars."

"Me, too," his sister added as she grabbed a Snickers.

Gail slipped the bar from her daughter's hand. "Uh, uh...no sugar until after breakfast."

"But we're on vacation," Kaylie argued. One look from her dad, and she quickly added, "Never mind. I'll eat it after breakfast."

Charlie Grace smiled. "Speaking of breakfast, it's all ready. Why don't you follow me over to the main lodge, then we'll get you some help with the rest of your luggage."

Aunt Mo had a table set in the dining room and soon served them what Jay quickly claimed was "the best breakfast he'd ever eaten." He turned to his wife. "No offense."

"No offense necessary," Gail assured him. "I wholeheartedly agree. I'm hoping Aunt Mo will share her recipe for that casserole. It was delicious."

About an hour after Charlie Grace got Jewel off to school, another car pulled in. An older man cut the engine, got out, and helped his wife from the shiny red Mustang. They introduced themselves as Harvey and Edith Cameron. Harvey was a retired assemblyman from New York's 27th District, which explained the couple's strong dialect and dropped Rs.

"We moved to Florida two years ago," Edith explained as she removed her hair scarf. "Both of us were ready to be rid of those winters."

"I hear you," Charlie Grace told her. "I've shoveled my share of snow."

"Thank you for offering to pick us up from the airport. We decided we'd like to have a car at our disposal, so we rented this beauty." He lifted his deeply veined hand and patted the hood of the convertible. "Makes me feel young again."

"You're not old, darlin'," his wife told him with a smile. "You're vintage. Like a fine wine aged just right."

The corners of the man's eyes crinkled as he smiled. "Well, at least no one can doubt my good taste in women." He pulled Edith into a shoulder hug and squeezed. "Never know...maybe I'll get lucky tonight."

Charlie Grace couldn't suppress her laughter.

She checked them into the cabin next to the Clarks and gave the sweet couple the same spiel, explaining the layout of the guest ranch and what to expect. "A tray of sandwiches will be available in the main lodge at lunchtime. Help yourselves whenever it suits you. Tonight, we'll be holding a welcome barbecue. I hope you like steak."

Dick's eyes lit up. "Now you're speaking my language."

The afternoon was filled with ranch chores. In addition to playing host to her new guests, she had to haul several loads of hay in the truck from near the barn to the corrals for the next feedings.

In the house, she met her dad's scornful expression. "How many times do I have to tell you not to put out that much feed? You want the elk to eat it all?"

"I'm going to have Gibbs cover the bales with tarps...if he ever gets back from town."

"Did you use last season's hay or the new crop?"

Charlie Grace held off a groan. With practiced patience, she turned and replied. "Last season."

"Did you check for mold? Sometimes you need to pull one of those bales apart and examine it close. We don't need sick cattle."

"The hay bales are not moldy, Dad."

"Are you sure? Because that's the feed we got from Buster. He leaves his cut alfalfa in the field for too long. The dew, coupled with the occasional rain, causes problems if you don't dry the hay out before baling."

She had heard this multiple times. "The hay is fine. And the price was right."

Her dad frowned. "Not if vet bills follow."

Charlie Grace rubbed her forehead. Why did she ever think she could win an argument with this man?

She moved for the cupboard, pulled out a glass, and filled it with water from the tap.

"Could you get me one of those?" her dad asked.

"Sure." She retrieved a second glass, filled it, and set it on the table before him.

He lifted the glass. "Who are all those people that showed up here this morning?" he asked, unable to contain his curiosity.

"A family from Utah and a retired couple from Florida."

Her answer met silence. The closest she got to a response was a slight grunt before he finally said, "Mo told me you had three guests coming in today."

She finished her water and set the empty glass in the sink. "Yeah, some guy is scheduled to arrive later this afternoon. It's slow, but a start." Wanting to cut the conversation short, she moved to his wheelchair and patted his shoulder. "I've got a lot to do, Dad. We'll talk later."

Outside, the Camerons sat in the Adirondack chairs nestled under the pines beside the river. Edith had a book in her hand and waved. Charlie Grace waved back.

The Carter kids were helping their father unload bikes from a rack on top of their SUV. Charlie Grace wandered over. "Looks like you're about to have some fun."

"The map shows there's a trail not far. Is that true?" Jay asked as he lifted one of the bikes to the ground.

"Oh, yes. There are many hiking trails, nearly all of which would accommodate bikes." She pointed in the direction of the south meadow. "If you follow the highway to the edge of those pines in the distance, there is a trailhead there that will take you along the river. It's an easy ride and beautiful." She directed her gaze to the children. "If you're lucky, you'll see some wildlife."

"Bears?" Kaylie asked, her face filling with concern.

"It's possible. Mostly brown bears, but a few grizzlies wander through. More often than not, at this time of the year, you'll find them in the higher elevations with their coy."

"Coy?" Kaylie asked.

"Their offspring." She turned to Jay. "There is a can of bear spray in your welcome basket in the cabin. I'd take it with you, just in case."

Charlie Grace let her face break into a smile. "There is a much better possibility you'll see elk and maybe a wolf in the distance. Keep your attention on the tops of the pine trees, and you might even spot an eagle."

"Cool," answered Kyle. "But I'd still like to see a big grizzly."

Charlie Grace's phone buzzed in her pocket. She excused herself and pulled it out to find Gibbs was calling. "Are you still in town?" she demanded. "I told you not to be long. We have..."

Before she could finish, Gibbs interrupted. "Flat tire. I was lucky to catch a ride back to town to the tire shop. When it's finished, I'll find a way back out to the truck and change it. Then I'll be back."

Charlie Grace groaned.

"Just a warning, from the looks on the tread, the tire may need to be replaced. Frankly, all four are worn to the point that the cords are showing through."

She did a quick calculation in her head. The operating loan was currently designated for other things, but she was used to robbing Peter to pay Paul. She'd have to juggle some expenses and make it work. "Replace all of them. But, Gibbs?"

"Yeah?"

"I don't need to tell you I'm on a budget."

"No worries. I got you covered. 'Ole Nigel down at the shop owes me. I'll negotiate a good deal."

She thanked him and hung up before returning to the Clarks. "Sorry about that."

"Trouble?" Jay motioned for Kyle and Kaylie to follow him as he wheeled the bikes toward their cabin.

She gave him a weak smile as she walked alongside. "Nothing that can't be handled." She invited him to pack up some of Aunt Mo's sandwiches to take with them on their biking adventure. "We have plenty of coolers in the kitchen for you to use. And don't forget...tonight we're having a cookout around the campfire. Bring your appetites, because Ford is cooking some rib eyes and baked potatoes. Aunt Mo made huckleberry cobbler and homemade ice cream."

"Yum!" the kids said in unison.

By midafternoon, her final guest had yet to arrive. She pushed back a niggle of worry, hoping he hadn't changed his mind. She lifted her iPad and checked his reservation which allowed cancellation. But without the requisite two-day notice, he'd forfeit his deposit. Still, she didn't relish losing the income for the three-day stay.

Before she could give the concern more thought, a vehicle turned onto the dirt lane from the highway and wound its way in her direction. The approaching car looked like a Lexus RX she'd seen recently in a magazine, a hybrid luxury sports utility vehicle. She groaned, knowing her dad was likely watching out the window and would have a lot to say about it later. He often voiced how this country was "going to hell in a handbasket" with all the climate control "nonsense."

While balance was always called for, anything that

protected the beauty surrounding them here in Wyoming was welcome, at least in her mind.

The car pulled up next to the Camerons' Mustang and cut the engine. Charlie Grace walked across the lawn to greet her new guest when suddenly her breath caught.

It was him...the guy from the Rustic Pine Tavern.

12

Charlie Grace fought to hide her surprise as she extended her hand to the handsome stranger. "Hi, I'm Charlie Grace, the proprietor here at Teton Trails. You must be..." She glanced down at her iPad reservation. "Nick Thatcher."

Deep dimples formed as he smiled back at her. "That's me." His voice was smooth, deep. Like good espresso. "Sorry if I'm a bit late. I ran into a bit of a roadblock on the way from Wilson —some grizzly and her cubs. Created quite the traffic jam."

She cleared her throat. "You drove from Wilson?"

"I'm here in Wyoming with a production company that is filming a television series set on a large ranch in that area."

"Like five thousand acres large?" she asked.

He nodded. "That's the one."

Charlie Grace knew it well. The Aspen River Ranch, one of the most prominent land masses in Wyoming. The ranch was built decades ago by a wealthy family from back east and was now owned and operated by the grandchildren. Plenty of famous people had stayed at the prominent destination, including a former president.

This wasn't the first occasion that filming had occurred at the site either. A documentary, several commercials, and even some movie scenes were shot along the scenic river.

She followed Nick to the rear cargo area of his vehicle, trying to remember how long it had been since she'd run a brush through her hair. "So, you're with the production company?" Like many of the locals, she was filled with curiosity. Early details surrounding the new television show had yet to be disclosed. The secrecy fueled the local rumor mill.

He lifted the hatch door before glancing back her way. "I'm the production designer, the one who translates the script into visual form. Before one inch of film is shot, I create a series of storyboards that serve as the film production's first draft. Those storyboards serve as the director's visual guide throughout the production and will be a template to follow during the editing process."

Charlie Grace let her gaze meet his, finding all that fascinating. "We're glad you're here with us here at Teton Trails."

Her heart skipped a beat, just as it had the other night. She couldn't help but feel a jolt of attraction. His wavy dark hair, chiseled jawline, and piercing blue eyes were impossibly charming. When he smiled, his eyes crinkled at the corners, giving him a friendly and approachable demeanor. Even more, there was a sense of confidence in his posture and the way he moved as he pulled his bags from the car that she found captivating.

He hoisted a large duffel over his shoulder and glanced around. "I'll never get used to this beauty."

"We like to say we live in God's blueprint for heaven."

His face broke into a broad smile, showing off those dimples again. "You got that right."

"Well, here, let me show you to your cabin." He followed as she led him past the main lodge. "We serve breakfast in the dining room daily at seven. We can also deliver a tray to your cabin if you choose. Sandwiches and accouterments are set out for lunch each day. Dinner is often outside by the campfire unless the weather forces us inside." She took a breath, knowing she was rambling a bit.

Nick continued to look around, taking in the surroundings. "Sounds good."

She led him across the lawn toward the guest quarters, well aware he was now watching her. "We want your stay to be comfortable."

They reached his assigned cabin, the last one in the row. The log structure had a front deck with an unobstructed view of the jagged Teton mountain range in the distance. She opened the door and handed him the key she'd tucked in her pocket, showing him inside.

He nodded his approval. "This is great."

She guessed him to be in his mid-forties and quickly glanced at his left hand to find no wedding ring. She immediately chastised herself for the move, remembering she wasn't some schoolgirl encountering the high school jock in the hallway.

Charlie Grace swallowed. "I—I hope you'll join us for our debut barbecue. Steaks and all the fixings out at the fire pit." She glanced at her watch. "Six thirty."

"Count me in. I'm starving." He tossed the duffel on the quilt-covered bed.

She bid him goodbye, wondering why she could barely breathe. Capri was right. This guy was a lot.

Capri picked up Charlie Grace's call on the first ring. "What's up? How's everything going on your big opening day?"

"Better than expected. All three guests have arrived, and so far, so good. Girl, you aren't going to believe who just checked in." Charlie Grace drew an energy bar from her stash in the barn and unwrapped it. "That guy."

"What guy?"

"The guy we saw at the Rustic Pine Friday night."

She could hear Capri's intake of breath across the phone. "McDreamy?"

"Stop calling him that...but yes, *that* guy."

"Why's he in town? I mean, you'd think somebody like that would be staying in Jackson. He doesn't strike me as the dude ranch type."

Charlie Grace pulled the wrapper down a little and took another bite, chewing while she answered. "He's with that production company. I found out they're filming at the Aspen River Ranch in Wilson."

"Ah, that confirms it, then. I heard a rumor that the new series would be located there. A very reliable source...Nicola Cavendish. We all know she knows everything."

They shared a laugh.

"What's the name of the show? No one seems to have figured that out, not even Nicola."

Charlie Grace stuffed the empty wrapper in her jeans pocket. "He didn't say. But, look...I've got tons of work still ahead of me, and I need to get back to it. Just wanted to share."

"Wait, before we hang up, should I warn Jason? He might want to know he has competition."

The comment irked her. "Oh, stop. It's nothing like that."

Capri laughed. "Just tell that to the dozens of people at the Rustic Pine who saw how he looked at you."

13

I t was only a matter of minutes before her phone started alerting her to incoming texts from Reva and Lila. No doubt Capri had immediately contacted them after she'd hung up, and they both wanted to know more about Nick Thatcher.

She slid her thumbs across the tiny keyboard as she headed for the house. "Looks like we don't need a newspaper in this town." When she failed to give them any more details, they both urged her to meet them as soon as possible.

"My place," Reva offered.

"I'll let you know. Right now, I'm just trying to keep my head above water," she told them. "And don't let Capri talk you into crafting some big story in your heads about this guy. I have a boyfriend."

"And lots of mustard," came Reva's quick reply, followed by laughter.

Little had changed since high school. Her girlfriends still got in her business, especially when it came to her love life. Or lack thereof.

Oh, she shouldn't say that. Jason Griffith was an extremely

nice guy...and dependable. He was handsome enough, with a well-groomed appearance and an easy smile, but something was lacking. When he looked at her...well, she felt nothing.

He spoke in a soft voice, never raising it above a polite murmur, and his words were always carefully chosen, never daring to stray into anything too controversial—or interesting. He was agreeable to a fault, always nodding along with her opinions and never offering any of his own. The times she'd tried to engage him and draw out some hidden spark of passion or curiosity, he had remained resolutely bland, content to exist in her presence without ever truly engaging with her.

So why stay with him? The answer was simple. Dating Jason had kept her from being alone. She never had to be the dreaded single girl showing up at dinner parties filled with couples. Jason was a good man, kind and considerate, but he lacked the fire and passion that she craved. She never went to bed at night thinking about him.

Her girlfriends knew her inside out. She might be satisfied with the status quo in her love life...but they were not.

"So, we get that you're busy," Reva said. "But here's the thing, you need some perspective. Plus, you can't keep us hanging. We're dying to hear all about your big opening. So, tomorrow night...my place?"

Knowing her friends would never take no for an answer, Charlie Grace gave in. "Okay, okay. Tomorrow night. But I can't stay long."

That evening, when it was just about time to gather out at the campfire, Charlie Grace slipped away for a quick shower. She reached for her favorite pair of jeans, then changed her mind, opting instead for a sundress in a cute print and a blue cardigan to ward off the evening chill, the sweater that complemented the lavender blue in her eyes. Next, she slid a pair of open-toe sandals onto her feet before pulling her long, auburn hair back into a ponytail. Her next task was to fasten tiny silver hoop earrings in place.

As a final touch, she spritzed a bit of her favorite cologne across her neck and stood back to inspect the image in the mirror. Satisfied she looked presentable, maybe even a little pretty, she headed out to join the others.

She hadn't reached the back door when her father's voice rang out. "Where are you going all dolled up like that?"

"I'm not dolled up," she argued. "You want to join us for the cookout? Ford is grilling steaks." She saw the sour look on his face. "Or, I can have Jewel bring you a plate," she offered.

He waved her off. "Nah, I can fix my own dinner."

Yes, he could. They had fixed a ramp from the back doorway onto the deck. Even in his wheelchair, her dad could reach the charcoal grill.

"Okay," she said. Before she moved for the door, she placed a kiss on the top of his head. "There's a chicken breast in the refrigerator."

He huffed. "Or, I'll just eat some oatmeal."

She held her tongue. If he wanted oatmeal, so be it. "Okay, goodnight, Daddy. Aunt Mo will be in later to help you to bed."

Charlie Grace hurried out the door and was met with a signature evening—warm air filled with the scent of pines, sagebrush, and just a hint of honeysuckle from the bushes her mother had planted next to the fence line. The setting sun was awash with a warm glow of orange and pink hues, leaving the mountains silhouetted against the sky and casting long shadows over the valleys below.

As she drew closer to the fire pit, the smell of wood smoke hit her nostrils, reminding her she hadn't eaten since that energy bar in the barn hours ago. She walked briskly toward the campfire, feeling the tickle of the blades of grass on her bare toes.

"Good evening, everyone! I hope you had a lovely first day

here at Teton Trails." She smiled. "And I hope you are all hungry."

"We had a great time today," Jay Clark announced. "We took a quick hike up to Hidden Falls. Amazing scenery."

"There were so many birds," his wife, Gail, added. "We even saw an eagle's nest."

Their son poked the campfire with a long stick. "Actually, Mom, it was a peregrine. Bald eagles are brown with white heads and tails. Peregrine falcons are similarly sized birds with dark blue bodies and white bellies. Their eye sockets, beaks, and talons are bright yellow. The white bellies of the falcons are barred, usually with brown, rust, or blue."

Charlie Grace grinned. "My, you know a lot about birds."

"He is especially into birds of prey," his father explained. "Has been since he was barely in school."

His sister spoke up. "I like hummingbirds."

"You do?" Charlie Grace asked.

Not to be outdone by her brother, Kaylie quickly added, "Did you know there are over three hundred species?"

Charlie Grace smiled with amusement. "I did not."

Satisfied, the little girl folded her arms and sat back in her lawn chair before continuing her animated conversation with Jewel, who had brought her Barbies to the event and was thrilled to have a playmate.

Charlie Grace turned to the older couple. "What about you two? Did you have a nice afternoon?"

Edith was quick with her response. "Oh, yes, dear. We both sat down on the edge of the river and read. So very relaxing."

A glance around the campfire revealed no sign of Nick Thatcher. Disappointment flooded Charlie Grace. Was he planning on skipping out on this evening's cookout?

Before the next thought fully formed, she caught a glimpse of him. He stepped out from the front door of his cabin onto his porch, then headed in their direction from across the lawn. He waved.

She stood with her eyes fixed upon him, taking in every detail of his appearance. He wore jeans and a casual button-down shirt with the sleeves rolled up enough to display his tanned forearms. For someone from California, he made a pair of cowboy boots look pretty dang good.

"Hey," he said in greeting as he neared.

"I wasn't sure you were coming," she said, trying desperately to hide how pleased she was to be wrong.

She made introductions and then turned to Ford. "And for those who haven't formally met our chuckwagon master chef, this is Ford Keaton. You won't eat better than what this man prepares." She patted his flannel-covered back. "This rugged, hardworking individual embodies the spirit of the American West. Lucky for all of us, he's about to delight our palates with the best grilled steak and cowboy beans ever tasted."

Ford adjusted the bandana tied around his neck and held up his wooden spoon with a hand calloused from years of working with cast iron pans and Dutch ovens over an open fire. "I hope you folks all brought your hungry tonight."

While everyone was dishing up, Nick appeared at her side. "I'm impressed. This is a first-class operation."

"Thank you," she said. "We have lots of hope for success." She pointed to the food line. "Shall we?"

He nodded and joined her by taking a plate and adding a thick slice of homemade bread baked in a Dutch oven pulled from the embers. He slathered on honey butter and took a bite before filling the rest of his plate. His eyes all but rolled back as he savored the delicious fare.

"You look like you just took a trip to heaven," she teased.

"I think that's fairly accurate," he told her. He added another slice before he moved on and added a scoop of the beans slow cooked with bacon and onions to his plate, along with a big helping of fried spuds.

She led him to the fire grate, where Ford lifted and placed a large rib eye, charred at the edges, onto Nick's plate next to the rest of his food. The weight of the meat caused Nick to blink. "I don't think I'll go away hungry."

Ford grinned. "That's the plan, young fella."

Reluctantly, Charlie Grace left Nick's side and played hostess to her other guests, making sure they all had what they needed.

When the meal was finished, Aunt Mo appeared with a large pan of huckleberry cobbler, fresh out of the oven. "There's homemade vanilla ice cream, too," she told them, pointing in the direction of a table holding a vintage hand-cranked wooden ice cream maker. She winked in Charlie Grace's direction. "I put Gibbs to work earlier."

A smile formed as Charlie Grace quietly mouthed, "Thank you."

Her aunt blew an air kiss her way.

While everyone enjoyed their dessert, Ford straightened up. When he'd finished scraping his pans clean and putting the dishes in the wash bucket, he grabbed his guitar from the back of his pickup. He hoisted one foot upon a stump, leaned over his knee, and tuned his instrument. "Any requests?" he asked.

Edith clapped her hands with delight. "Do you know 'Home on the Range'?" She turned to the others. "I once heard that song in a John Wayne movie in a scene much like this."

"You bet, ma'am." Ford strummed his guitar and sang as the flames danced and crackled in the fire pit. His fingers moved nimbly over the strings, producing a rich and soothing melody that filled the cool mountain air. The guests sat transfixed by the music and the rustic ambiance of the campfire. Soon, they were singing along as he played, even the kids.

As the light faded, the colors of the sky deepened, shifting to shades of violet and deep blue. The first stars began to twinkle into view as the last remnants of sunlight gave way to pitch black blanketed with piercing tiny lights.

Charlie Grace looked across the campfire and found Nick Thatcher watching her. She dared to smile, and he smiled back.

She sat back and tried to take it all in, memorizing and storing every detail in her heart. All her hard work and plans culminated in this...an evening she hoped her guests would never forget.

She knew she wouldn't.

14

R eva opened the door to find her three best friends standing on her deck. "There you are," she said, waving them inside. "You're late."

"You mean busy," Lila corrected. "Doc Tillman went home early this afternoon. Left me to tend to a Labrador with stomach issues and a cat with conjunctivitis. Not to be indelicate, but I think he had a bad case of hemorrhoids."

"The Lab?" Reva asked.

Lila shook her head. "No, Doc Tillman."

"Ew...and you know this how?" Capri handed Reva a tray of homemade enchiladas. "Mom sent these."

Reva lifted the casserole dish from her hands. "Extend my gratitude. This sure beats my bowls of chips." Despite her affinity for good food and her expensive kitchen, she wasn't known for her culinary skills.

Charlie Grace tossed her jean jacket over the sofa back. "Let's get back to why Lila knows her boss had hemorrhoids."

Lila shrugged. "I saw him take the lidocaine cream we use when cows have prolapsed rectums into the bathroom with him."

"Double ew!" the other three said in unison.

Reva laughed and set the casserole dish on the stone countertop. "I don't envy the man you'll someday marry. With your lack of filters, dinnertime around your table will be very interesting."

Lila shrugged a second time. "Yeah, sorry. I forget how squeamish people get." She grabbed a chip from the bowl. "And I'm never getting married again."

"Never say never," Charlie Grace told her.

"Oh? And what about you?" Reva moved for the refrigerator and pulled out a pitcher of margaritas. "Last I heard, you'd sworn off matrimony as well."

Charlie Grace rested her hand on the back of a barstool. "Well, that's different."

"Right," they all said, laughing.

Capri narrowed her gaze to the wall across the room. "Did you get a new piece of art?"

Reva nodded. "It's a Paula Baucum original, an artist from Texas. Her pour paintings have such incredible movement. I love them."

Reva's house was a showcase of mountain chic décor. While relatively simple in terms of architectural form, she'd paid a lot of attention to luxury details. Warm tones, local stone and timbers, inlays of metals, and leather furnishings created an inviting interior. Soaring open-beamed ceilings and walls of floor-to-ceiling windows melded her home and nature...the feature she most loved. She especially appreciated the unobstructed view of the river and the Teton Mountains.

Reva poured the margaritas and handed the stemmed glasses to her friends. "So, let's get to the reason we're all here." She turned her focus on Charlie Grace. "We need the scoop on your handsome new guest."

A tiny smile formed on Charlie Grace's face. "Well, he is handsome; I'll give you that."

"And how long do you get to enjoy looking at Mr. Handsome?" Capri asked. "Is he staying long-term?"

"He's only registered for three days." Charlie Grace kicked off her boots and folded onto the sofa, tucking her legs underneath her. "Besides, I don't have time to gawk. I've got a lot of important things to do." Even as she said it, her eyes twinkled.

"Ah...well, enjoy the scenery while you can," Reva urged while grabbing herself a Perrier water from the refrigerator. "No harm in that."

Charlie Grace blushed and waved off the comment. "Do I need to remind you we're no longer girls roaming the halls of high school? We're grown women with responsibilities, jobs, and people who depend on us. Remember?" She turned to Reva. "You're the mayor of this town, for goodness' sake."

"We're women who still have red blood running through our veins," Reva reminded.

Lila sat on the floor near the sofa. "Oh, that's rich...coming from someone who hasn't dated in well over a year. All our love lives are fairly dim at this point."

True, Reva thought. The idea of dating was low on her list after Merritt.

"Back to the subject." Reva unscrewed the top off her water bottle. "Tell us more about...what's his name?"

Charlie Grace took a sip from her margarita. "His name is Nick Thatcher. He must come from money because the internet says he..."

"You looked him up on the internet?" Reva exchanged glances with the others. "That seems significant."

"Internet research takes a lot of time for such a busy woman," Capri teased.

"Oh, stop." Charlie Grace set her glass on the table. "Yes, he seems like an interesting guy. But that doesn't mean there are romantic implications. Besides, like everyone in this town, I care about tourism and what that new television series will mean to our town."

None of them looked entirely convinced.

Lila leaned back against the sofa cushion. "Okay, so what did you learn?"

"Well, he's quite the muckety-muck in Hollywood, with a long and illustrious career as a production designer. He's worked on some major projects." She named several well-known movies. "He even won an Oscar."

"Wow!" Capri said.

Reva whistled, echoing the sentiment. "Impressive."

"What's a production designer?" Capri asked, reaching for a chip.

"Nick says he is the one who plans each scene. He calls it 'storyboarding.'"

Reva returned to the kitchen, slid the enchiladas into the oven, and adjusted the temperature control. "My office has been inundated with people stopping by with questions about this show. Understandably, there would be a lot of curiosity, especially since everything seems so hush-hush." She swiped a cloth over her granite countertop. "That seems to fuel speculation."

"Yeah, Nick didn't disclose many details—and I certainly did not want to pry—but apparently, filming is going to be out at the Aspen River Ranch in Wilson."

"Figures." Capri reached for the pitcher to refill her glass. "The people who own that place are connected."

Reva joined them in the living area and sat in the chair across from the sofa. "Many locals relish the potential tourism this production will bring to the area, but I'm on board with the concerns being expressed."

"What concerns?" Charlie Grace asked.

"No one wants long-term growth in terms of people flooding into the area to live...or worse, building second homes that drive up the property values and taxes and then remain vacant when the owners return to California."

Lila nodded. "Exhibit A: Sun Valley, Aspen..."

"Jackson Hole," Capri finished. "I've said before, bring on the summertime tourists. That's good for all of us. But, we don't need more taxes. My profit margins are set. I'm not keen on raising my prices to cover increases."

"Yes, that's the sentiment I most often hear," Reva confirmed. "Along with questions about how to become an extra in the show."

They all laughed.

"Hey." Capri sat up straight. "Now that we have an in with Charlie Grace, maybe we can all be in the production. Add film star to my resume."

Lila's face brightened. "My daughter would die to have her moment of fame."

Charlie Grace slowly shook her head. "Well, I don't know about any of that. Tell you what...you're all welcome to come out to Teton Trails and pitch the idea yourselves." She grinned. "Have at it."

15

T he next morning, Charlie Grace stopped at her dad's bedroom on her way down the hall. Hearing movement from behind the closed door, she knocked lightly. "Dad? You up?" She waited and heard another shuffle. "Do you need anything before I head out to feed?"

He grunted loudly. "No, I don't need your help."

She sighed. "Okay, then. I'll be back after a while." With determination, she moved through the kitchen and out the back door, not bothering to stop and make coffee. It'd been a late night with the girls, and she'd let herself stay in bed about twenty minutes longer than normal. The decision meant she'd have to get a move on this morning. No time to dawdle, not even for the much-needed caffeine.

Charlie Grace loved the early hours of the morning, just before the sun broke over the horizon when the world still slept and a hushed stillness settled over everything. It was as if the entire landscape held its breath, waiting for the first light of dawn to pierce through the darkness and awaken the day...a moment of raw potential, full of untold possibilities.

She moved across the yard, enjoying the crisp, cool air.

Upon reaching the barn, she unlatched the door and moved inside the dark interior stable. For several seconds she stood on the concrete floor in the comforting stillness, breathing familiar leather and liniment-scented air before her fingers instinctively moved to the panel to the right. She pulled the lever, and light immediately flooded the tack room.

After knotting her hair at the back of her head and securing the clip a bit tighter, she drew a blue bandana from her back jeans pocket and tied it at her neck. She made her way through the wash bay and headed for the stalls, where she grabbed a grain bucket from the nail on the wall. Against the opposite wall were several grain sacks. She opened one and filled the container, making a mental note to remind Gibbs to order more grain. They were already getting low again.

Charlie Grace lifted the heavy pail and made her way to the horse stalls, where she dumped the grain into the individual plastic feeding containers, stopping to rub the nuzzle of each horse before moving to the next. When she was finished, she glanced at her watch, noting that Gibbs was late...again.

Outside, the sky had lightened slightly, signaling she needed to hurry and finish up. Soon, it would be time to get her daughter up and ready for school.

As she stepped outside the barn door, a distant motion caught her eye. She stopped and squinted, straining to make out the figure heading for the river.

It was him...Nick Thatcher.

He knelt on the ground with one knee and pointed his camera lens toward the stand of quaking aspen trees along the bank of the river. She stood mesmerized, watching him take shots of the tiny silver-dollar-shaped leaves dancing in the faint light of morning. He crouched and pointed his lens up toward the top of the trees, popping off several shots. Then he knelt for several more before he stood and traded out his lens.

Nick turned, saw her, and immediately stopped what he

was doing. His face broke into a smile, and he waved for her to join him.

Embarrassed to be caught watching him, she pulled the gloves from her hands and headed his way.

"Good morning," she said. "I see you're a photographer?"

Dimples appeared at the corners of his mouth as he smiled. "My job includes lining up shots for the big camera, but personal photography has been my passion for as long as I can remember. There's something about capturing a moment in time, freezing it forever in a single image, that never fails to captivate me. It's not just about taking a picture; it's about telling a story. I love the way a photograph can evoke emotions and memories, transporting the viewer to a different time and place." He put the cap on his lens. "For me, photography is a way of seeing the world in a different light, of noticing the beauty in the mundane and the extraordinary. Whether it's the way the sunlight filters through these trees or the expressions on people's faces, every scene is a potential masterpiece waiting to be captured."

He grinned. "Sorry...I didn't mean to ramble."

"No, that's...well, that's amazing. I only wish..." She paused, feeling heat flood her face. She waved off her thought. "Oh, never mind."

"No, what?"

"I...it's that I used to love to take photographs. My mother gave me a camera when I was twelve. A Canon."

"You don't take pictures anymore?"

Charlie Grace shook her head. "Nah, I got busy. Never seemed to have time to pursue photography." She paused. "I still have it. The camera my mother gave me." She looked at him, pulled in by those eyes. "She died. I was fourteen."

"I'm so sorry."

"Yeah. It was an extremely hard time in my life. Everything changed. I had a lot more to do around here, and then one thing led to another. I got engaged, married...became a mother. Divorced." Her voice drifted.

She couldn't help but feel a sense of melancholy wash over her. It wasn't that she was unhappy with her life; she loved this ranch, her daughter, and her friends. But as she looked back on her younger years, she couldn't help but feel a twinge of regret. There was a time when she had been so passionate about life, so eager to explore the world and all it had to offer.

Somewhere along the way, the mountain of responsibilities that came with adulthood had taken over, leaving little time or energy for the passions of youth. Now, when she looked in the mirror and noticed tiny wrinkles forming around her eyes, she realized that time was slipping away from her. She longed to recapture that sense of wonder and enthusiasm she felt in her youth, but it seemed like an impossible dream.

"Life happens," she muttered, feeling the weight of the admission.

She'd once been so carefree. But after years of carrying so many responsibilities, she'd turned cautious, weighing every decision and assessing how her actions might impact those around her...especially those she dearly loved. It was exhausting at best. At worst, she often wondered if she even knew who she was anymore.

Where had that girl gone?

Charlie Grace looked up and caught his gaze. Something shifted within her. He seemed to read her thoughts and see right through her into the very depths of her soul. It was both exhilarating and terrifying to be seen so completely by another person. A stranger even.

But as she looked into his eyes, she saw no judgment. Only understanding.

"I get it," he told her. "I've learned sometimes you need to cut the strings to keep from becoming a Pinocchio."

Nick uncapped his camera, then reached and brushed a strand of hair back from her face. "Do you mind?"

Her breath caught. Feeling self-conscious, she shook her head no.

He unclipped her hair and watched it fall free from the restraint. Smiling, Nick pointed his lens.

Click, click, click.

"I hope you didn't think that was creepy," he said. "It's just that...well, I wanted to capture this moment, the way the sunlight reflects off your hair."

Her hand instinctively went to the long curls lying across her shoulder.

He withdrew the camera strap from around his neck and held his camera out to her. "Here. Try it."

She hesitated. It had been so long since she held a real camera. This particular model was no point-and-shoot, but way more complex...and more expensive. As she looked into his eyes, all she saw was trust. How could she refuse?

With trembling hands, she took his camera, feeling the weight of it in her hands, and for a moment, she was transported back to a time when photography made her so happy. As she brought the camera to her eye, she felt a thrill of excitement, as if she were reconnecting with an old friend.

"My, this lens is amazing," she whispered as the world beyond shifted into focus. She scanned the horizon, landing on a bluebird with its bright, cerulean blue plumage that was almost iridescent in the morning sunlight.

Charlie Grace adjusted the lens with her fingers, zooming in until she could see the smooth lines of the small bird's sleek feathers and its pointed beak perfectly designed for snatching insects out of the air.

She snapped a shot and grinned. Then took another.

The bird went airborne and flitted from tree to tree, moving with a grace and fluidity that was almost otherworldly.

Charlie Grace lowered the camera and sighed. "Did you see it? The bird?"

Nick nodded. "I am stunned by the beauty of this place you get to call home."

She reluctantly handed him his camera. "Thank you. That made my morning. And it certainly has prompted me to pull my camera back out."

"I hope so," he told her, smiling.

"Well, hey...I have a daughter I must get ready for school. See you at breakfast?"

He again nodded. "At breakfast."

Charlie Grace couldn't keep the smile from her face as she backed away, already feeling a twinge of disappointment that duty called, and this chance encounter was at an end.

"Okay, yeah...see you at breakfast." She slowly took a couple more steps back.

Nick's lips curled into a gentle smile. He watched her intently. She could see a hint of mischief in his eyes, his gaze warm and playful.

It made her feel special.

She quickly glanced at her watch. "Oh, my goodness! I'm late." She gave him a quick wave, then turned and broke into a full run toward the house. With every pounding step, she carried his smile with her.

16

Charlie Grace sprinted across the grass, then bolted up the stairs and across the wooden deck. She pushed the door open and instantly heard giggling coming from the kitchen. Hurrying in that direction, she picked up Jewel's backpack as she passed the sofa and tucked it under her arm.

"What's going on?" she asked, surveying the scene. Her uplifted spirit immediately withered.

Gibbs held their daughter in the air. Her feet dangled, and she laughed as he tickled her neck with his scrubby unshaven chin. Her father sat in his wheelchair, his eyes filled with amusement as he drank his coffee.

"Jewel," she shouted, not meaning for her voice to sound so harsh. "Why are you still in your pajamas? You have to meet the bus in less than twenty minutes." She pointed down the hallway. "Go! And be quick."

Her daughter's face sobered, and she scrambled to her feet to obey, glancing back at her grinning dad with a forlorn look.

Charlie Grace turned her ire upon her ex-husband. "Did she even eat breakfast? Or, was she too busy playing with you?"

Gibbs held up open palms. "Wow, somebody drank sour milk this morning. And don't glare at me. I just got here."

"Yeah, noted." Charlie Grace frowned. "Where's your truck?"

"I woke up to a dead battery. So, a friend dropped me off."

"A friend." She turned and pulled open the refrigerator door, plucked a container of yogurt from the shelves, and slammed the door closed with her hip. "She couldn't get you to work on time?"

Charlie Grace turned to face her father. "I warned you this would happen. I'm still doing all the chores. Only now, we have him on the payroll. Makes perfect sense." She groaned and jerked open the utensil drawer with enough force to rattle the silverware inside.

She plucked a spoon out, then slammed the drawer shut. "It's not like we're rolling in dough these days. If we're laying out cash for some help...I'd like some!"

"Calm down," her father warned. "Nothing gets solved by screaming at the top of your lungs."

Charlie Grace whipped around. "Just once, I'd like you to be on my side. It takes far too much energy to fight you both." She turned and jabbed her finger in the air at Gibbs. "You're fired."

Gibbs' eyes widened. "Oh, don't go getting all out of sorts. I told you...my battery died."

"I hired him," her father firmly stated. "I'm the one who will fire him."

Charlie Grace's eyes narrowed with scorn. "Seriously?"

"Calm down," Gibbs echoed. "You're getting yourself worked up over nothing."

"Nothing? My entire adult life, I've had to knock up against the two of you. I wish someone had clued me in when I carried the bouquet down the aisle, I was stepping into a marriage of three people."

Gibbs leaned against the counter with his arms crossed. "Cut it out, Charlie Grace. You know that's not true. Your dad..."

"My dad wanted a son, and you fit the bill. End of story."

Charlie Grace felt herself losing it. Rarely did she voice her frustrations. Especially at this level...and volume. But she'd had it!

Her father set his mug down on the table with a loud thud. "Listen, Charlie Grace. I get that you're upset, but you're going overboard. I don't..."

Unshed tears suddenly burned at the back of her eyes as thoughts appeared of all that she'd missed in life. She swallowed and forced herself to lower her voice. "Listen? Dad, that's all I've done since Mom died. Did you ever stop to consider what I wanted? The sacrifices I've made? Do you think it's a party running this ranch and trying to keep things afloat after you..."

She saw the wounded look that crossed his eyes and stopped. Why allow the truth to tear him to shreds? He was still her father. Despite being a stubborn cuss, he was family.

"Fine," she murmured, defeated yet again. "Gibbs stays." She turned her gaze on Gibbs. "But three strikes, and you're out. You hear me? No more excuses. No more tardy appearances. No more playing in the kitchen with Jewel while I do chores without your help." In a feeble attempt to regain some semblance of authority, she straightened her shoulders and looked him dead in the eyes. "I'm docking your pay for showing up to work nearly two hours late. No arguments."

Gibbs grinned and reached for a piece of hair that had fallen across her cheek. "Okay, sure. Won't be late again. And, you can dock my pay."

She slapped his hand away. "I wasn't asking for your permission. By the way, you can drive Jewel to school this morning since she just missed the bus." She nodded toward the window. The yellow school bus pulled to a stop at the end of the lane and honked. Seconds later, when no one appeared, Donna Hatfield put the bus in gear and drove away.

"Daddy's taking me to school?" Jewel appeared at the entrance to the kitchen, beaming. She wore a pair of pink denim pants and a lavender top bejeweled with tiny rhinestones in the shape of a puppy. It was apparent she'd tried to braid her own hair, unsuccessfully.

"C'mere, puddin'." Charlie Grace extended her arm and motioned for her daughter to move closer. She sat in a chair at the table and positioned Jewel before her, then pulled the rubber band from the bottom of one of her daughter's pigtails. She used her fingers to comb the strands in place and quickly re-braided her hair before doing the other side. "There you go." She patted Jewel's bottom. "Be good and study hard. We'll see you after school." She thrust the yogurt and spoon into her daughter's hand before turning to Gibbs. "Make sure she eats this on the way."

Her ex-husband raked his hand through the top of his disheveled brown hair. "Uh, Charlie Grace?"

She sighed. "Now what?"

"Could I borrow your vehicle? I mean...I don't have wheels right now."

Before Charlie Grace could respond, her dad reached into his back pocket and pulled out a set of keys. He tossed them into Gibbs' hands. "Take the ranch truck."

"Thanks, Clancy." Gibbs put his hand on Jewel's shoulder and guided her to the door. "Be back as soon as I can." He turned to Charlie Grace. "Uh, would you mind saving me some of Aunt Mo's breakfast? I'm starved."

Charlie Grace grimaced. "Just go!"

As soon as the door closed, Charlie Grace moved for the counter, picked up the wet dishrag, and wiped off the table.

Her father lifted his coffee cup, allowing her to swipe underneath it. "Charlotte Grace, what's eating you?"

"We're not having this conversation, Dad. I already said my piece."

"Gibbs is no longer your husband, and you're still cawing at him like a disgruntled wife."

She tossed the wet rag into the sink. "I'm not cawing at him. I'm simply holding him accountable."

"He's not a bad man, Charlie Grace."

"No, Gibbs is not a bad man. He's a man who never grew up, a man who could never keep his pants on, and a guy who let his wife shoulder all the responsibility while he played."

She immediately chastised herself. Why was she even engaging? They'd had this conversation a million times. Her father would never see things her way.

He was right about one thing. Throwing a fit about her life was fruitless. If things were to change, she was going to be the one to make things different. Maybe Nick was right...she had some strings to cut.

"Hey, do you remember that camera Mom bought me when I was a kid?"

"Vaguely," came his reply as he wheeled himself over to the coffee pot to top off his cup.

"Well, I'm going to find it."

"Yeah?"

Charlie Grace lifted her chin. "Yes. I'm going to find that Canon, and I plan to start taking pictures again."

Her dad grunted. "Is that so?"

"Yes, that's so. This morning, someone unknowingly urged me to start looking at life through a new lens." She moved for the back door. "And, from here forward...I plan to do just that."

R eva hung her aqua sweater on the peg in her office, straightened the front of her sleeveless dress, and made her way to the windows overlooking Main Street. She waved at a passerby before she took a seat behind a worn, wooden desk—a desk that had seen over fifteen mayors.

Serving as mayor of Thunder Mountain had not been something she'd aspired to. Her law practice, located two doors down the street, was more than enough to keep her busy.

Reva had built an eclectic practice, with clients that included ranchers dealing with federal grazing issues, couples seeking a divorce, small mom-and-pop businesses that needed purchase and sale agreements, or loan agreements like the one she'd recently negotiated for Charlie Grace.

She'd also been the attorney of record for the city when Hank Peters suffered his fatal heart attack, right here at this desk. She stepped up and covered his duties and was surprised at the overwhelming support to make the effort official. She was the sole, and successful nominee, in a special election, vowing to serve only one term. That was three terms ago.

Service was her personal hallmark, and she loved serving

the residents of Thunder Mountain. Yet, there were a few downsides.

One of them rapped at her open door.

"Yoo-hoo. Do you have a minute? I have something very important I need to discuss with you."

Nicola Cavendish strode toward her with a look of concern on her face. She wore a hot pink pantsuit with a blouse ruffled at the neck...and an attitude. She didn't wait for a response before she took a seat.

Reva sighed. "Hello, Nicola. What can I do for you?"

Nicola tossed her purse onto the neighboring guest chair. "I am the voice of many who wish to express our intense displeasure over a matter critical to our way of life here in Thunder Mountain. Or, should I say, a threat to our way of life?"

Reva leaned back in her chair, listening intently to Nicola's concerns. "Care to expand?"

She braced herself. Nicola had a tendency to exaggerate and blow things out of proportion.

"It's about that television show being filmed nearby. From what I understand, there have been leaks on the internet suggesting the show is high drama, with extreme violence and..." She leaned forward and lowered her voice. "...and onscreen *sex*."

"I understand your worries, Nicola," Reva said, trying to reassure her and diffuse the situation. "Unfortunately, there is very little the mayor's office can do to influence the type of production planned. The city simply does not have that kind of control. Despite any moral issues, some believe there are potential benefits that this television series could bring to our area. It could draw in new tourism and boost our economy. That could result in new businesses and strengthen local commerce. Who knows, maybe it will show the world what a great community we have here."

Nicola huffed. "Exactly what we don't want. We don't want

to become another Sun Valley or Sundance, overrun with rich celebrities who don't care about our way of life. Our town has always been a quiet, humble place, and we don't want to lose that."

Reva nodded, now more aware of the source of the rumored concerns she'd already been hearing. Nicola Cavendish was as ruffled as her blouse over the matter.

Reva understood the sentiment and even shared the concern. "I understand the influx of wealthy individuals could have both positive and negative effects on our community. But I also believe it is possible to balance the potential benefits of increased tourism and economic growth with preserving our town's character and way of life. I assure you that I will take all this into account when making any decisions regarding the matter. But I think it's even more important that we all acknowledge the extent that I'm officially limited when altering the course of what is happening with that production. The primary film location isn't within the city limits."

"Did you know that one of the executives is staying out at Teton Trails? Does Charlie Grace know that?"

Reva took a deep breath. She wasn't going there.

Nicola leaned closer to the desk. "And let me tell you, Reva. I've heard some of these shows can be downright disrespectful to the people and places they film. They come in with their big cameras and bright lights, disrupting the peace and quiet. Who knows what kind of people they'll bring in as crew? Those Hollywood types do drugs. We don't want any of this kind of trouble in Thunder Mountain, now, do we?"

Reva nodded in appreciation. "Of course not." She stood, a signal that she was ending the conversation. "Nicola, I assure you that nothing is higher on my list of priorities than protecting Thunder Mountain and its residents. I've noted your concerns. Let me give the matter more thought. Until then..."

She circled the desk and extended her hand. "Give Wooster my best. Will I see you both at the oyster fry next week?"

Nicola reached for her bag, placed the strap over her folded arm, and stood. "Of course, I'll be there. Wooster is the chairman of the event. Do you have your tickets yet?" She dug into her purse and pulled out a pack of bright blue paper coupons bound in a rubber band.

"I'll take a dozen," Reva told her. She retrieved some cash from her purse and pressed the bills into Nicola's hands.

The woman's face finally brightened. "Excellent. As you know, the funds raised go toward our children's literacy program at the library." She removed the rubber band and counted out the correct number of tickets, then set them on the corner of Reva's desk. "We'll see you there then."

"Yes, I'll definitely see you there," Reva said.

Just before Nicola exited through her office door, she stopped and turned back. "And you'll give what we've discussed some serious consideration?"

Reva nodded and promised again that she would.

18

Charlie Grace tried to stuff her disappointment when she served breakfast with Aunt Mo and discovered Nick Thatcher absent from the table. Even more so when she mentally calculated he would be checking out tomorrow.

She set a large platter of biscuits on the checkered table-cloth next to a bowl of cream gravy. "So, how did everyone sleep?"

Edith Cameron placed a napkin on her lap. "Oh, like a bear in hibernation."

"Yes," her husband agreed. "We were worn out after taking a long drive yesterday through Yellowstone Park."

"With the top down," Edith added. "We saw so many wild animals. Harvey and I got a little nervous when we encountered a herd of buffalo along the road in what the map called Hayden Valley."

"Yes, but what could we do? I wasn't about to pull over to put the top up on the Mustang."

They both laughed. Edith poured herself some orange juice. "It was a grand adventure."

Charlie Grace turned to the family from Utah. "Looks like you are scheduled to leave us today. I hope you enjoyed your time with us here at Teton Trails."

Kyle motioned for his mother to add a second scoop of scrambled eggs to his plate. "We had a blast!"

His sister picked up her fork. "My favorite was horseback riding. Mom and Dad promised we could come back next summer."

Charlie Grace beamed inside. That was just the feedback she was hoping to hear. "We would love to have you back again."

After breakfast, she left Gibbs to help clear the table. He'd balked at the idea after returning from taking Jewel to school, but she'd held up her hand. "You're really going to argue after you missed your morning chores?"

He dropped the issue, grinning back at her. "No. You're the boss. Besides, it'll give me time with this beautiful lady." He playfully popped Aunt Mo on the behind with a rolled-up dish towel.

"Oh, stop." Aunt Mo swatted at the towel, laughing.

Charlie Grace retreated to the office, where she opened the reservation system. She had a couple arriving tomorrow morning who were on their honeymoon. She scrolled down and stopped. A slow smile dawned as she saw a pleasant surprise.

Nick Thatcher had extended his stay...indefinitely.

REVA FINISHED REVIEWING the minutes from last week's city council meeting and closed her laptop. The review didn't take long since the only agenda item had been a discussion surrounding an application for approval of a snow cone stand on the corner of Main and Ninth. While concerns were voiced about the hours of operation, all the dissenters quickly conceded when it was learned the applicant was the high school flag corp, and all proceeds went to fund travel to a state color guard competition in Laramie.

Reva stood to collect her things, planning to head out for lunch, when her office door flew open. She looked up to find Capri standing there looking completely undone. "I need your help," she said, brushing a loose curl off her face.

"What is it?"

Capri closed the door behind her and motioned for Reva to sit. She then slid into one of the guest chairs. "It's my stepdad, Dick. He's at Moosehead Tavern. I'm afraid he got some bad news this morning. He wouldn't tell Mom or me what it was. I only know he received a disturbing phone call and left the house without a word." She paused, trying to collect herself. "I waited a few minutes, then followed. He parked in front of the Moosehead, and I watched him go inside."

"Oh, dear," Reva murmured. Dick was a regular attendee at her AA meetings and had been sober for a good many years. He'd even helped out as a sponsor in a pinch. She tucked the strap of her purse upon her shoulder. "Thanks for letting me know. You stay. I'll go see what's up."

Capri, who was the toughest of all her girlfriends, couldn't hold back her emotions. Her eyes teared up. "Thanks, Reva. I knew I could count on you."

Minutes later, Reva stepped into the dimly lit bar. She steeled herself against the smell of cigarettes and alcohol that blanketed the air inside as she scanned the room, her eyes darting from one patron to the next, searching.

Then she saw Dick slumped over at the end of the bar, his hand wrapped around a glass of amber liquid.

She made her way over to him, her heels clicking on the tiled floor. He didn't notice her at first, lost in his own thoughts. She cleared her throat, and he turned to look at her.

"Hey," she said softly. "Mind if I sit down?"

Dick shrugged, and she took the seat next to him. She glanced at the glass in his hand, noticing the way his knuckles turned white as he clutched it tightly.

"Bad day?" she asked, knowing the answer already.

Dick let out a bitter laugh. "You could say that."

They sat in silence for a few moments, the noise of the bar buzzing around them. She could see the internal struggle he was going through, the battle between his desire for a drink and his commitment to his sobriety.

"You know," she said finally. "I've been there. I know what it's like to feel like the weight of the world is crushing you, and all you want to do is forget about it for a little while."

He looked at her, his eyes flickering with a glimmer of reconsideration.

"But the thing is," she continued. "We both know from experience that the drink in our hand won't fix anything. It won't make bad news go away. It'll just make it harder to deal with tomorrow."

Dick sighed, his grip on the glass loosening slightly. "You don't understand."

Reva placed her hand on his arm. "I know it's hard," she said gently. "But you've come so far. You've worked extremely hard to get where you are. Don't throw it all away now."

He nodded slowly, and she could see the determination returning to his eyes. "I got bad news today."

"Do you want to tell me about it?" she urged.

Dick sat silent for several seconds before he turned and looked at her. "I've got cancer."

Reva couldn't help the quick uptake of breath as she struggled to absorb his news. "I am so sorry, Dick." She gave his arm a little rub. "What's the prognosis?"

"Liver. Guess all those years of drinking finally caught up

with me. Stage four...so there ain't no way a transplant or anything is gonna change things."

"How long?" Reva gently asked.

"Only the good Lord knows for sure, but the doctors in Cheyenne tell me six months to a year, maybe even less."

Reva's mind immediately went to her good friend, Capri. For years, she'd struggled with her stepdad's alcohol addiction. He hadn't been what they called in AA—a fun drunk. He was often mean, and his inebriated comments often bit into the adolescent girl's self-esteem, especially when she attempted to rescue her mother from his verbal assaults.

Thankfully, Dick had finally sobered up years ago after his fourth car accident, where he put a young family in the hospital. The event served as the catalyst for some major changes in his life, not just in his drinking but in how he interacted with his family and friends. Soon, the old Dick gave way to a new version—a man who quietly gained the respect of others.

Not only was Dick Jacobs Capri's stepfather...he was Reva's friend.

She gently reached and removed the glass from his hand and pushed it aside before laying her head against the older man's shoulder. "You won't be alone, Dick. You have a family— and an entire town—who loves you and will help you through this."

"And that includes me," she whispered while squeezing his arm. "I promise."

19

R eva pulled her Escalade to a stop near the Jenny
Lake Visitor Center parking lot. She pointed to a
blue bike locked up on the rack. "Bingo."

Charlie Grace followed Lila out of the car. "Not a surprise
that this is where she'd come."

Reva nodded. The four of them had made an unspoken
pact years ago. When one of them was in crisis, the others
would drop everything and help. This wasn't the first time
they'd found Capri at her favorite spot to run when she was
hurting and needed time to think.

Lila waved for them to follow as she headed for the trailhead lined with purple lupine. Reva pressed the button that
lifted the hatch gate. She retrieved a backpack and slid one of
the straps over her shoulder, then closed and locked her vehicle
before joining the others.

The hike was a short thirty minutes. As they made their
way along the trail, they passed by a crystal-clear stream that
flowed down from the mountains. The water cascading over
rocks created a soothing soundtrack.

"Okay, here's where we turn," Lila announced and stepped

off the path, winding her way through a dense forest of spruce and fir. The air was rich with the scent of pine needles and fresh mountain air. Occasionally, one of them had to duck a low-hanging branch.

They'd walked less than ten minutes when they reached a rock outcropping that offered a panoramic lake view. Against the background of the stunning vista sat their friend, cross-legged and her back to them.

"Capri?" Reva ventured as they drew close. "You okay?"

She turned, her voice choked with tears. "You know, I used to hate him. He wasn't the kind of guy who gave you a lot to like. But there was this one time when I was eleven..." She paused and turned back to the lake. "He took me fishing. I didn't want to go. I was scared of him. But he didn't often take no for an answer back then."

Lila, Reva, and Charlie Grace folded down beside her. Reva opened the backpack, took out bottles of water and some Hershey candy bars, and passed them out.

Capri unwrapped her chocolate bar. "He brought me right down there." She pointed to a spot along the lake where the thick blanket of trees gave way to a shoreline of sand and gravel. "He said it was 'our' spot and claimed that it was the best fishing in all of Wyoming."

Her face broke into a tiny smile. "Turned out he was right. We caught nearly a dozen large rainbow trout that day. He shared his secret...he'd thread the usual earthworm on his hook, but he added a tiny piece of colored marshmallow. Brought a whole bag and let me eat most of them." She smiled at the memory.

Her eyes clouded. "He's the only dad I've known." She took a bite from her bar.

Her friends all nodded in support. Reva stuffed the wrapper from Capri's hand in the backpack. "How's your mom taking the news?"

"Mom always seems to roll with the punches, even when the force knocks her off her feet."

"I suspect her faith carries her through these kinds of things," Lila offered.

Capri let out a tiny huff. "They say God never gives more than you can handle, but he's loaded up my mother's tray far too many times." Her expression stiffened. "Yet, I've never met a stronger woman or anyone happier. Go figure."

Charlie Grace picked at a piece of grass. "No doubt she has calluses on her knees from praying for her wayward husband. There is no better example of redemption than your stepdad. How he turned his life around...well, it's remarkable."

Reva quickly agreed. "Dick exemplifies someone who reaches out to people with shattered spirits...because he knows what it was like to be broken. You are right to mourn this news."

They sat in silence for several moments before Capri turned her attention from the water to her girlfriends. "It's okay," she said, shrugging off her friends' concerned looks. "I mean, it's not okay, but we're going to get through it."

Capri brushed a piece of grass from her pants. "We talked about all this, and my mom and I will be there for Dick every step of the way," she said, trying to sound more confident than she likely felt.

Reva placed her hand on Capri's arm. "We would expect nothing less. But we know this is going to be hard for you, too."

Capri looked down at her lap. Tears pooled at the corners of her eyes. "I guess I'm just scared," she admitted, her voice trembling. "I don't know what the future holds, and I hate that feeling of uncertainty."

Her friends leaned in, listening intently as Capri shared how she intended to cover all the medical expenses. "He doesn't have great health insurance," she told them. "No matter how I urged otherwise, he seemed to think buying my mom the better policy was the way to go. And I doubt he ever qualified for a life insurance policy. So, yeah...there will be those other expenses. I'm glad I have the funds, and my mom won't have to worry about how to wrangle their depleted bank accounts."

Lila finished her chocolate bar and tossed her wrapper into Reva's hands. "Well, we're here for you. We can all drive Dick to medical appointments."

"Or sit with him," Charlie Grace added. "Give your mom a break when she needs one."

"The thing is," Reva said, gazing at her friend with a look of encouragement. "You are not alone. We're right by your side, and you can count on us to help in every way possible."

They all exchanged knowing glances, determined to be the pillars of strength their friend would need in the coming days.

"Thanks," Capri murmured. "I love you all so much."

Before anyone could respond to her unusual show of sentiment, Capri abruptly stood. She pointed to a nearby tree with a fishing pole leaning against the bark. "So, now that we've got my emotional crisis covered, who's up for fishing?" She lifted a bag for them to see and smiled. "I brought the marshmallows."

20

The start of the following week dawned with a full roster of guests due to arrive. Charlie Grace was surprised that word had already spread in such a short time since Teton Trails' opening. Lots of people were calling to make reservations, and summer was already filling up.

Still, bidding goodbye to her very first set of guests was bittersweet.

The Clarks departed, telling her they had the best time ever. They were so happy with their stay that they booked again for next summer, which elicited cheers from their twins. Dick and Edith Cameron couldn't wait that long. "We'll be back in the fall," Edith told her. Both families left glowing reviews on her website.

Charlie Grace had been reluctant to add staff until she knew revenue would cover the additional expense. When reservations started rolling in, she quickly realized she'd be foolish to put off hiring someone to help with making up beds, doing laundry, and relieving Aunt Mo of some kitchen duties.

So, as soon as breakfast was over and Jewel was on the school bus, Charlie Grace headed to town to place a classified advertisement in the help wanted section of the newspaper. Albie Barton, the editor, still printed and hand-delivered papers. Just last year, he'd folded on his stubborn resolution and began offering an additional online issue. "Only weekly," he warned. "The daily issues will remain in print. We're still old school here at the *Thunder Mountain Gazette*—and proud of it."

As soon as she parked and got out of her truck, Nicola Cavendish spotted her from across the street at the Cowboy Cafe, where she was having coffee at an outdoor table with Dot Montgomery and Oma Griffith. "Yoo-hoo!" She waved her arms wildly, trying to get Charlie Grace's attention. "Charlie Grace! Wait up."

Charlie Grace groaned inside and forced a smile, watching as Nicola looked both ways for passing cars, then scurried across the street. "Hey, Nicola," she said as the banker's wife approached.

"I am so glad I ran into you," she said. "I'm sure you've talked with Reva, and she told you of my concerns?"

"No," Charlie Grace started walking for the newspaper office, forcing Nicola to follow beside her. "What concerns?"

"Is it true one of the executives from the film company is staying out at Teton Trails?"

Charlie Grace braced herself. She wasn't about to discuss her guests with anyone, especially Nicola Cavendish. "I'm sure you can appreciate that I can't..."

Nicola waved off her comment before she could complete her sentence. "Oh, yes. I understand privacy issues and all that. I'm just asking if you can confirm that one little bit of news."

"I'm afraid I really can't." The shade at the newspaper office window went up, signaling Albie was inside. "Look, I've got to go, Nicola. But I'll see you at the oyster fry later this week?"

Nicola lifted her chin. "Certainly." She looked at Charlie Grace full-on. "Maybe I'll drop by Teton Trails sometime. Everyone is raving about your new guest ranch and all you've done out there. I'd love to see it."

Charlie Grace groaned for the second time. "Sure, anytime," she told her banker's wife. No reason to upset the cash cart. She bid Nicola goodbye as quickly as possible and turned for the newspaper office.

Inside, Albie was leaning close to his computer monitor, looking over the top of his reading glasses. He glanced up as she entered. "Oh, Charlie Grace. I'm so glad to see you. Do you know anything about that new artificial intelligence everyone is talking about? I saw on the news last night that people say it may put writers out of business...even editorial writers."

The concerned look on his face was enough to make her try to reassure him. "No one can replace you, Albie. Can computer robots write about our oyster fry here in Thunder Mountain or about how the late spring snowpack will affect the start of baseball season? You're good," she assured him.

He didn't look convinced. "Well, maybe I'm safe. But this world is changing far too quickly, and not always for the better," he said, turning from his computer. "Now, what can I help you with?"

Charlie Grace explained her need to hire help. "I was hoping to get a classified ad set up before the next issue."

"Well, it's not often I take business away from the paper, but I think I can save you some trouble and a little expense," he told her. "My niece is arriving next week. My sister lives in Seattle. She's a single mom, working late shifts at the hospital to make ends meet. Her girl needs to earn some money to help with college expenses. I told Nancy to send her my way, and I'd find her something."

"Oh? So, she's what...nineteen?"

"Twenty-three, actually. She's going to graduate school in

the fall. And at the top of her class. She'll have scholarships, but anything extra comes from her own earnings. She'll be here through Labor Day. That might work out perfectly for you. Summer is likely going to be your busy season."

Charlie Grace thought it over. She wasn't expecting to hire someone without first meeting the candidate. Yet, she trusted Albie. "Okay, sure. You say she arrives tomorrow?"

Albie beamed. "Yes, her name is Lizzy Cayman."

"I can only pay minimum wage," Charlie Grace warned.

"That's fine," Albie assured. "She'll do you a good job."

Charlie Grace nodded. "Okay, then. Tell her she's got the job. Give her a day to get settled, and then send her out to the ranch, and we'll put her to work. Thanks, Albie."

"Thank you." He made his way from out behind the desk and extended his hand. "I can't wait to call and tell her."

Charlie Grace had to pick up groceries before she returned to the ranch. She stopped at the Western Drug and General Store and hurried up and down the aisles, plucking the items on Aunt Mo's list from the shelves—among them eggs, bacon, laundry soap, and toilet paper. Wholesale deliveries from Jackson were scheduled to start next week. Good thing, these retail prices were gouging her pocketbook. She made a mental note to adjust her budget and moved to the checkout lane, where she placed her items on the conveyor belt, then pulled out her business bank card, trying not to choke when she saw the total.

Bob Simpson, the owner, appeared from the back, his arms loaded with plastic shopping baskets. "Hey, Charlie Grace. How are you today?"

"Fine," she told him, frowning as she handed over her bank card.

Bob looked between her and the clerk. "Fran, let's give Charlie Grace the business discount."

"Business discount?" she asked, puzzled.

"Yes, Fran. You know...the business discount."

She slowly nodded. "Oh, yeah. The business discount." Her face broke into a smile as she punched a button on the register. The total immediately reflected much less.

Charlie Grace glanced between them. "Thank you, but that was totally unnecessary."

Bob grinned at her. "It's nothing. Just a little boost for your new business. We're all hoping Teton Trails is a huge success."

"Well, the gesture is truly appreciated. I expect you both to come out to the ranch and join us for a steak cookout soon."

They promised they would take her up on the offer.

After giving Bob and Fran a hug, Charlie Grace raced home, unloaded the items from her truck, and delivered them to Aunt Mo. "So, it looks like I found a new hire to help us."

"Oh?" Aunt Mo shelved the items in the pantry. "That was quick."

"Albie's niece is arriving in town tomorrow. She needs a summer job before attending graduate school."

Aunt Mo lined the packages of toilet paper next to a stack of towels, fresh from the dryer. "Well, I hate to admit it, but the help is welcome."

Charlie Grace pulled a bottle of water from the refrigerator and removed the lid. "Both a blessing and a curse. I never expected us to fill up so quickly. According to our online reservation system, we barely have an opening until after the Fourth of July."

Aunt Mo beamed. "I'm not surprised. You've worked hard, baby girl. All the credit for this success lands directly in your lap."

"Good try," Charlie Grace interjected. "We both know this guest ranch could never have gotten off the ground without you." She took a sip of her water and put the lid back on the bottle. "Who knew we'd be full up after only a week?"

Aunt Mo's face drew into a warm smile. "Everyone believed you'd have success but you."

"And Dad."

Aunt Mo focused her gaze and clasped Charlie Grace's elbow. "What do you mean?"

"Dad wasn't exactly behind all this. He most certainly didn't believe in me."

Aunt Mo frowned. "Oh, honey. He's not one bit surprised. Why do you think he groused so? He's scared of everything changing."

"I didn't have a choice. Things had to change, and he places the blame squarely in my lap."

Aunt Mo pulled her into a hug. "He'll come around. You'll see."

When Charlie Grace had finished helping Aunt Mo in the kitchen, she took the clean bedding and changed beds. A couple was arriving later this afternoon. Another family was coming in this evening. And several more guests were scheduled to be here in the morning.

She had no more than finished up the cabins when a Jeep wound its way up the lane and parked. Out climbed a middle-aged couple.

Charlie Grace brushed the hair from her cheek and headed in their direction.

"Welcome to Teton Trails," she said, greeting her new guests with a wave. "Hope you didn't have trouble finding us."

The man looked to be in his fifties. He was tall, had short-cropped brown hair, and wore jeans and a button-down in a nice shade of blue. "No trouble at all. The map on your website was very helpful." He moved to the passenger side and helped his wife from the vehicle. She was a pretty woman with mid-neck length hair the color of a Hershey chocolate bar. Her eyes were warm and friendly when she smiled.

"We are so happy to have you with us. I'm Charlie Grace, the main proprietor."

He shook her extended hand. "Tom Strobbe. And this is my wife, Ava Strobbe."

The woman laughed. "That still sounds so strange. I've been a Briscoe for nearly my entire life," she confided. "Tom and I just got married in Hawaii."

"Oh, congratulations!" Charlie Grace's face drew into a puzzled look. "And you left Hawaii for your honeymoon? Sorry, but that feels a little backwards to someone like me."

"We live there...on Maui, actually," Tom explained. "We thought we'd honeymoon stateside, in the mountains. We've just spent a week in a cabin near Glacier National Park. We'll stay a week here and explore Yellowstone and Teton National Parks, and then our plan is to head south to Ouray, Colorado."

"Tom talked me into going on a two-day backcountry Jeep excursion while we're in Ouray. Way out of my comfort zone." She smiled up at him with the adoration of a newlywed.

Charlie Grace learned that Tom and Ava lived and ran a pineapple plantation in Maui called Pali Maui. Ava had four children and three grandchildren. "This is my second marriage," she explained.

Tom threaded his fingers with hers. "Mine as well. We look forward to spending the rest of our lives together."

Ava quickly agreed. "Yes, it's never too late in life to be happy."

Charlie Grace swallowed, silently hoping the sentiment was true. They were so lucky to have found each other.

"What about you? Are you married?" Tom asked as she showed them to their cabin.

"I was."

Ava climbed a couple of steps onto the porch leading to the front door where they'd be staying over the next few days. "Ah, well...I hope you are as lucky as Tom and me and find someone special."

Unbidden, an image of Nick Thatcher waiting at the end of the aisle formed in her mind. The idea startled her. She shook the thought from her mind, mentally chastising herself for such a ridiculous—and unwelcome—notion.

She quickly diverted her attention back to her guests. "Here, let me help you get settled."

She aided Tom and Ava with their luggage before giving the newlyweds a brief tour, guiding them over to the main lodge, to the stables, and to the area where they hosted the campfire dinners. "You won't find more authentic Western cooking than what Ford Keaton serves up," she told them. "His fried spuds and onions will have you begging for seconds."

Ava grinned and linked arms with her new husband. "I get that. There's nothing like local cuisine. Back home, my best friend, Alani, delights luau guests with kalua pork that can bring tears to a grown man's eyes."

"So, the website says this is a working ranch?" Tom asked.

Charlie Grace nodded and told them the history of the ranch, how her ancestors had homesteaded the acreage so many years back. "We're delighted to have an opportunity to share this land with people who will love it as we do."

"Everything here at Teton Trails is absolutely wonderful and exactly what we hoped for," Ava told her.

Charlie Grace's phone buzzed in her pocket. She excused herself and stepped away to take the call. It was Jason.

"I hope I'm not interrupting anything," he said when she answered.

"Well, the truth is...I am checking some guests in. Can I call you back?"

There was a short pause. "Sure. I'll be here."

She thanked him and closed off the call, then returned to her new guests. "I'm sure you're ready to tackle seeing the sights. Please let me know if there is anything you need. Dinner will be at six right here."

"Excellent," Tom said. He turned to Ava. "I think we're going to unpack and then go for a drive."

Charlie Grace suggested a quick trip north along Jackson Lake. "You might even loop down through Colter Bay. The drive only takes about an hour. Of course, add an extra hour for stops. You're sure to see a lot of wildlife, and there's no prettier place for photos. Especially if you stop at the various overlooks."

"Thanks, we'll do just that," Tom said.

Charlie Grace bid her new guests goodbye and headed for the house. She hadn't taken time for a shower earlier this morning and desperately wanted to freshen up before the barbecue tonight...for the guests and no one special, she told herself.

From her closet, she pulled out a pretty daffodil-colored top she'd picked up in one of the clothing boutiques in Jackson a few weeks back. Unlike most women, she wasn't a fan of shopping. Thankfully, her girlfriends could be counted on to help her select things that framed her figure and enhanced the faint lavender hue found in her eyes.

After her shower and getting dressed in the top and a matching skirt, she gazed at her reflection in her bathroom mirror. The image that stared back confirmed what she'd often been told. She was blessed with a great complexion and nice features. She didn't have to resort to cosmetics to accentuate her looks. Yet, despite all that, Charlie Grace couldn't resist the temptation of her bathroom drawer, where she searched for a touch of mascara and lipstick to enhance her appearance.

Satisfied with the final result, she studied herself in the mirror once again and couldn't help but feel pleased with what she saw.

She didn't need any man to validate her. But deep down,

she couldn't deny a secret little thrill that came with the possibility of catching a particular guest's eye.

About an hour before the scheduled dinner time, she was delighted to see Nick Thatcher's car driving up the lane, approaching the parking area. He pulled into a vacant space and cut the motor. Seeing her, he waved and headed her way.

"So, I was just going to grab my camera and hike down to the end of the meadow. I hope to catch a few shots down along the riverbank while we have this fabulous light. I know you're likely busy with everything, and it looks like you're dressed for dinner, but if you can slip away..."

"I'd love to. And I'll change."

The minute she said the words, she chastised herself. She had a mountain of things she should be doing and had no business joining him. Still, the immediate elation she felt was nothing she wanted to quash. "Yes, let me run to get my camera."

He grinned. "You found your mom's Canon?"

She nodded with enthusiasm. "It was right where I'd stored it away."

Charlie Grace exchanged the skirt for a pair of jeans, grabbed her camera, and was back in a jiff after telling Aunt Mo she'd be gone for a short while.

"Go, sweetheart," her aunt urged. "It won't be a problem."

She leaned and gave the older woman a little kiss on the cheek, feeling slightly breathless. "Okay, if you're sure. I mean, Ford has everything under control."

Aunt Mo was more than amenable to her taking a few minutes for herself. "Yes, we're good. Go. Everything here's fine."

With that blessing, she joined Nick on the porch of his cabin, now wearing a cute pair of jeans and boots, with camera in hand.

"Ready?" he asked, looking at her with an intensity that made her shiver.

"Yeah, let's go."

As they headed across the meadow in the direction of the river, Charlie Grace couldn't help but feel a sense of anticipation mixed with trepidation—a fact that begged a question.

She had a business to run. A daughter. A boyfriend.

What in the world had gotten into her?

21

W
ith her camera slung around her neck. Charlie
Grace walked with Nick through the marsh grass
along the bank of the river that meandered
through the northern end of the property.

"This evening light is amazing." Nick's voice was reverent
with a tinge of excitement. "I was afraid we might be too late,
but these long shadows are just what I was hoping for."

"Look over there!" she said in a hushed voice. With the
majesty of the Teton Mountains looming in the background,
she pointed to a moose standing at the water's edge, grazing on
the opposite bank from where they stood.

Nick's face immediately brightened. "Let's move closer and
try to get a good shot," he said, already adjusting his camera
settings.

They crept closer, taking care not to disturb the moose. Its
fur was a deep brown, thick and shaggy, almost velvety to the
touch. The animal's ears twitched as it listened for any signs of
danger.

Charlie Grace motioned, and they crouched low near a rock
cropping a safe distance away.

She watched as Nick opened his camera case, pulled out a lens, and quickly fastened the piece of equipment in place. Charlie Grace lifted her own camera and pointed in the direction of the sight before them.

A sudden movement caught her eye. Her breath caught as a small figure stepped out of the tall marshes. As the figure drew closer, she realized it was a baby moose, only a few weeks old.

Nick saw it, too, and began clicking off shots in rapid succession. Charlie Grace did likewise.

The sight of the little creature was heartwarming, its small size and clumsiness a stark contrast to the imposing figure of its mother. The baby moose wobbled on unsteady legs, trying to keep up with its mother's steady pace as the larger moose moved along the riverbed.

The click of her camera shutter and the whir of the auto-focus worked together to create a sensory experience Charlie Grace hadn't experienced in a very long time. She clicked off several shots and then adjusted the focus, the depth of field, and the shutter speed until everything was just right. She took several more shots.

Her heart pounded at the thrill of captured images, the moments in time frozen by her actions. Her hands shook with excitement as she aimed her Canon for an extreme close-up of the moose and its baby, marveling at the texture of their fur, the shine of their eyes, and the details of their fuzzy velvet-like ears, all while trying to capture the perfect composition. The moose and her baby seemed oblivious to their presence, which allowed her to zoom in close enough to catch every intricate detail.

She dropped her camera to review the images and felt a rush of accomplishment and pride, knowing she had just captured something extraordinary.

Suddenly, Charlie Grace could feel Nick's eyes on her. Her

heart skipped a beat. She tried to concentrate on her images, but she couldn't help stealing a glance at him from time to time.

"What?" she finally said.

Nick's face drew into a slow smile. "I couldn't help but admire the way you see the world through your lens."

Charlie Grace felt the heat of his steady gaze.

"Do you always blush so easily?" he teased.

Despite his playful words, the look in his eyes was filled with deep respect. She saw a softness there that made her feel seen and understood in a way she hadn't before. It was as though he was seeing her for who she truly was—not as an ex-wife, a mother, a ranch worker who struggled to keep everything afloat—but as a woman filled with wants and the need for adventure.

It made her feel vulnerable but also exhilarated.

Despite her immediate reservations—and there were a lot of reasons she should run from these feelings—she couldn't help but be drawn to him. How he looked at her with admiration and tenderness made her feel special.

She hadn't felt special in a very long time.

Nick seemed to realize what she was thinking. "Look, I can't go back without telling you how much I've enjoyed this. I hope we can do it again...very soon."

She swallowed. "Yes, I'd like that." A timid smile pulled at the corners of her lips. "I'd like that very much."

22

The cookout was in full swing by the time Charlie Grace and Nick returned. "Wow, that's quite a group," Nick said. "And the food smells wonderful."

Charlie Grace was startled to see more than the number of guests currently staying. Not that she minded. Teton Trails always had the welcome mat out.

"Yoo-hoo! Hello." Nicola made her way in their direction, waving. She wore a western-styled snap shirt in a bright floral print and cowboy boots in a shade of turquoise. Her arm was looped with her husband's as she pulled him along. "I hope you don't mind. I called out to see if I could drop by, and your dad answered. He said you were hosting a big shindig tonight and invited us to join."

The news surprised her. Her father didn't think too highly of Nicola Cavendish, often referring to her as the "drama queen of Thunder Mountain."

"Well, we're glad you're here," Charlie Grace fibbed. Knowing exactly why the woman had barged into this event, she turned to her companion. "Have you met Nick Thatcher?"

A sly smile sprouted on Nicola's face. "No, I don't believe

we've had the pleasure." She extended her manicured hand. "Although we've heard a lot about you, Mr. Thatcher."

"Oh?" Looking amused, his eyebrows lifted. "And what have you heard?"

Nicola leaned forward and lowered her voice. "Word has it you are one of the producers for that television show."

"Well, actually, I'm the production designer for *Bear Country*," he corrected.

"I read you've won an Oscar." Nicola elbowed her husband. "Isn't that right, Wooster?"

Wooster immediately extended his own hand. "I'm Wooster Cavendish. I manage Thunder Mountain Savings and Loan in town." He retrieved a business card from his wallet and thrust it into Nick's hand. "Feel free to reach out if you have any financial needs. We are a full-service bank..."

Before he could finish his pitch, Nicola elbowed her husband a second time. "Oh, honey. I'm sure Mr. Thatcher does business with some big financial institution in Los Angeles...or China." She laughed at her own bad joke.

Charlie Grace sighed. "Look, I hope you'll excuse us. We're just getting back and..."

Nicola noticed the cameras in their hands. "Oh? You've been out together?" Her lips pursed. "Isn't that nice?"

"We stumbled upon a moose and its baby," Nick offered. "Got some tremendous shots."

Charlie Grace reached for Nick's elbow. "We'd love to chat more, but I'm pretty sure Nick is starving. Let me get this poor man a plate." She didn't bother to wait for Nicola's response before pulling Nick toward the spot where Aunt Mo was busy helping dish up plates of food for a line of guests. "I'm so sorry, Aunt Mo. Let me help you."

Her aunt waved her off. "No worries, honey. It's all handled. Besides, Ford carried the load tonight." She looked at Nick.

"Get you a plate. You're not going to want to miss out on a plate of those ribs."

Nick held up his camera. "Let me put this away and get washed up." He glanced at Charlie Grace. "Save me a seat?"

She beamed. "You bet."

"Mommy! Where have you been? I've been looking everywhere for you!" Her daughter parked her hands on her hips.

Charlie Grace laughed. "You have? Well, I'm sorry." She held up her camera. "I was taking some photographs. Just wait until you see my shots of this momma moose and her baby."

"I want a camera!" Jewel exclaimed. "Then we can take pictures together."

Nick grinned. "That's a wonderful idea. You look like a great future photographer." Forgetting his intention to return to his cabin, he motioned Charlie Grace's daughter to a table and sat, offering the chair next to him. "Here, take a look." He handed his expensive camera to her.

"Oh, be careful," Charlie Grace warned. "Don't break it."

Jewel rolled her eyes. "I won't break it, Mom."

Suddenly, Charlie Grace felt a hand on her back. She turned.

"Hey," Jason said. "Sorry, I'm late."

Charlie Grace blinked a couple of times, now recalling her invite extended through his mother, Oma. She'd seen her in town earlier that day.

"I tried to call you," he reminded.

It dawned on Charlie Grace that she'd totally forgotten to call him back. "Oh, yeah. I meant to return your call, Jason. I'm sorry. I got busy."

His arm went around her waist, and he leaned and kissed her forehead. "No problem."

Charlie Grace's insides froze. Nick watched intently, unspoken questions clearly expressed on his face.

She had trouble finding her breath. "Uh, Nick. This is Jason Griffith."

Jason smiled widely and pushed his hand forward. They shook. "Welcome to Thunder Mountain," Jason told him, oblivious to the tension. "Hope you enjoy your stay."

"Here you go, sir." Jewel handed the camera back into Nick's hand. "I want one just like it." She turned to her mother. "I'll do extra chores to earn the money."

Charlie Grace barely managed a smile. "We'll work something out, sweetheart. In the meantime, would you take Mommy's and put it in her bedroom? Be careful with it," she warned, handing the camera over.

"I will," Jewel called over her shoulder, already running for their house.

Nick pointed toward his cabin. "Well, if you two will excuse me, I need to stash this away and wash up. I'm starving."

She didn't quite catch the look on Nick's face, but could his expression be...disappointment?

She watched him walk across the lawn for several seconds before turning to Jason. "Again, I'm sorry I forgot to return your call."

"No, worries. Let's get you some ribs."

With her plate filled, Charlie Grace made her way to Ford. "You outdid yourself tonight," she told him with great affection.

The older man's eyes twinkled, showing deep creases at the corners. "There's few things I enjoy more than serving up a good meal to fine folks."

Tom and Ava Strobbe, the couple from Hawaii, joined them. "Well, these fine folks certainly enjoyed your meal." Tom patted his stomach. "I am stuffed."

"Yes," Ava said. "I couldn't eat another bite."

Ford let his face break into a playful frown. "Not even a little homemade vanilla ice cream with huckleberry sauce...again, homemade?"

Ava groaned. "You're killing me."

Ford's face broke into a wide grin. "You won't be sorry," he promised. He placed a hand on Ava's back and led her to where Aunt Mo was now dishing up scoops into large white bowls. "This lady needs some dessert," he said, pointing to the large ice cream scoop in the older woman's hand.

Charlie Grace set her plate down and hurried to her aunt's side. "I'll get that, Aunt Mo."

Her beloved aunt quickly shut down the idea. "Eat! I've got this."

Grateful, Charlie Grace picked up her plate and headed for an empty spot at one of the tables set up in the yard. Jason came over and bid her goodnight. "Sorry to leave early," he said. "But I promised Mom that I'd bring her some of Ford's ice cream." He raised a plastic bowl covered with a lid. "Can't let it melt."

"You should have brought Oma with you," she chastised. "She was more than welcome."

"I told her that, but she begged off. Her arthritis was flaring up and she thought a good hot bath with some Epsom salts might do the trick." He leaned and kissed the top of her head. "See you at the oyster fry?"

She nodded. "Of course. Goodnight, Jason."

He patted her shoulder. "'Night, Charlie Grace."

She'd barely raised her fork and knife when she saw Nick heading her way. The sight caused her heart to squeeze. "Hey, there you are," she said, granting him a timid smile. "Sit." She pointed to the place next to her. "Did you get full?"

He returned the smile. "More than. You serve up amazing meals out here at Teton Trails."

Jason's pickup wound down the lane. He honked and stuck his hand out the window, waving back at her.

She waved in return, then turned her attention back to Nick. "Thank you again for today. I loved every minute."

Without taking his eyes off Jason's truck, her new friend let out a slight cough. "So, are you and that guy..."

"Friends."

He slowly nodded. "I see."

She drew a deep breath, no longer all that hungry. "Do you have a friend?"

"I used to." Nick turned his attention to the darkening sky, where a few stars were beginning to appear. "It's difficult to maintain a relationship when you travel as much as I do," he explained. "She wanted more."

"I'm sorry," Charlie Grace offered, strangely relieved.

"Don't be. I believe that when two people are meant to be together, it all works out. And, when it doesn't...." He let his voice drift. He breathed in and asked what he seemed to really want to know. "Do you love him?"

The directness of his question shook her to the core. She stammered to respond, hoping to soft coat the sad truth of her relationship with Jason. "No, not really. Don't get me wrong. Jason is a nice guy. We've dated a long time." She lightly fingered the tines of her fork. "I'm divorced."

"Gibbs?"

"Yeah, how did you know?"

"He let me know the first night I met him." Nick brushed an ant from the table. "He seemed pretty proprietary."

Charlie Grace groaned. "Don't even get me started." She gave Nick a brief rundown on the demise of her marriage and the reasons behind the divorce. "Gibbs is a trademark wanderer."

"His loss." Nick gazed at her intently. "And, in my opinion—he's a fool."

Her breath caught. He was flirting. Flirting!

Admittedly, it felt good to have someone like Nick Thatcher interested. No one ever talked about how thrilling it was to be looked at in the way Nick was staring at her right now. It was a bit heady—this infatuation. The excitement of wondering what the other person would say next, the delight of knowing that person was looking at you and liking what they saw, the rush of it all. She felt like a schoolgirl.

A schoolgirl with a boyfriend. She had a lot to sort out.

She quickly reined in her giddy emotions. "Tell me more about you," she urged, wanting to learn more about this stranger whom she found intriguing. "Where'd you grow up?"

"I was raised in Orange County, California—not far from Disneyland."

"Ooh, I always wanted to go to Disneyland."

He shook his head. "I've been dozens of times. You're not missing anything." He let his attention drift to the sky filled with stars. "You have everything, and more, right here. This place is magical."

"It is," she agreed.

"L.A. is nothing like Wyoming. It's crowded and hurried. Everyone seems frantic to make their way to some unknown destination." He rubbed at his chin. "My parents owned a florist shop. I worked there after school as a kid. When I was old enough to get my driver's license, I drove the delivery truck." His face grew reminiscent. "That's how I paid for my first camera. A second-hand Nikon I found down at the pawn shop. I don't know why, but I was drawn to photography from the time I was a small kid. I spent countless hours experimenting, taking pictures of everything from my pets to the trees in our backyard. The joy of capturing a moment in time and freezing it forever was a feeling unlike any other."

"Yeah, I get that," she said.

Nick leaned his arms on his knees. "I grew older, and my love for photography grew as well. I'd go to the library after school and study books on different techniques and the styles and works of famous photographers. Eventually, I realized that I wanted to take my passion to the next level, and I enrolled in

UCLA and got into a program that focused on developing tech-nical skills, but also the critical and theoretical aspects of the medium." He paused and rubbed at the back of his neck. "Sorry, I'm boring you."

"No, please. Go on," she urged.

"Well, in addition, the program encouraged students to engage with the wider Los Angeles art community. That's how I met the head of a small production company who was willing to take on an eager intern who wanted nothing more than to absorb everything he could."

"Herb Nelson," she murmured.

"How did you know...?"

She felt heat rise to her cheeks. "Your acceptance speech at the Oscars. I looked you up on the internet," she confessed, a fact that seemed to please him.

In an attempt to divert attention from her blunder, she glanced around. "Where'd everyone go?"

"I think they all wandered inside the lodge," he told her.

She looked at her watch, amazed at how much time had passed. Her full plate still sat on the table before her. She pushed her uneaten dinner aside and dared to meet his gaze. "I find myself a bit jealous of your life. Of all the traveling—new places, new people. It must be thrilling."

"What about you?" he asked. "Did you always want to run a ranch?"

Charlie Grace shrugged. "I don't know. There was never a plan, really." She explained how her ancestors had made their way west on the Oregon Trail. She told him how her great-grandfather had homesteaded the ranch and how the property had been passed down several generations. "My dad was in an accident. I've always helped out, but that's when I stepped up and took over."

"What happened?" he asked. "To your dad, I mean."

Charlie Grace's throat thickened like it did every time she

talked about that day. She fixed her eyes on the smoldering embers in the firepit. "It was a summer day four years ago. Dad was repairing one of the fences when he decided he needed to work the new rescue horse he'd taken in. A wounded horse is predictably hard to manage. It could very well take several men to load the horse safely." She paused, searching for the fortitude to continue. "Dad is known for being an ornery cuss—and a stubborn one, at that. I told him to wait for Gibbs, who was due to arrive to pick up Jewel. He refused to follow my advice."

"Ah..." was all Nick could find to say. "I think I can see where this is going."

She nodded. "Yeah, the horse reared upon loading, and his hoof landed in a bad spot. Split Dad's head open," she said, placing her hands on the table in front of her. And then, lowering her voice, added, "I was frantic."

Nick gently brushed the top of her folded hands with his own. "I'm so sorry."

"The doctors weren't optimistic, and when he woke up from the coma, he was paralyzed from the waist down." Charlie Grace's insides shook as she remembered the pain of the event. "Dad was always such an active man, always on the move. The accident left him wheelchair-bound, and he hates every minute of it. He's angry and resentful that he can't do the things he loves, like riding his horse or tending to the cattle."

Charlie Grace paused, her throat now tight with emotion. "It was a difficult time for us. We were struggling to adjust to the new normal. But it was hardest on Dad. He felt like his life was over, like he was useless. He's still filled with anger for not being able to make things the way they were before the accident." Her sigh held a hint of defeat. "Unfortunately, he often takes his frustrations out on the people closest to him."

"On you?" Nick asked.

She quietly nodded. "On me."

Charlie Grace fell silent, lost in her memories. The fire

crackled in the background, casting a warm glow over the table, but Charlie Grace felt a chill in her bones. The story was painful to recount.

Nick squeezed her hands. "It must be rough on you."

They were both quiet for several minutes, unsure what to say next. Finally, Nick broke the silence. "Charlie Grace, I'm at a point in my life where I've learned that life is not a spectator sport. I no longer sit on the sidelines hoping things turn out how I want. I've learned to pursue what will make me happy, even if the path ahead looks messy."

She looked up, a bit confused.

"I know things are complicated. I don't want to add to that. But I'd like to continue to get to know each other. I want us to be friends." He let the statement hang in the air, waiting for her response.

"Friends," she repeated, pondering their earlier references to that word.

"Yes, I'd like to be friends." He gave her hand a meaningful squeeze. "No pressure. I simply prefer to be direct. I want to spend more time with you." He ran his finger down one of hers. "And see where that leads."

23

C harlie Grace could barely wait for her Friday night get-together with the girls. She had a lot to process after her evening with Nick. She couldn't quit thinking about all that had transpired, rehearsing over and over in her mind everything that he'd said...and the things she'd left unsaid.

Her mind was like the tilt-a-whirl ride at the annual carnival, dipping and going 'round and 'round. Despite what she wanted, she had so much to consider. So many roadblocks to simply jumping off into exploring the possibility of a new and exciting relationship.

She had her daughter to consider. And Jason. The last thing she wanted was to hurt him.

She needed to get her head on straight—and that most often happened when Capri, Reva, and Lila helped her gain perspective.

"There you are," Lila said, waving her inside.

Charlie Grace pulled off her cowboy boots and set them by the door. "Sorry I'm late," she said, making her way into the living room where the others waited. "Mmm...do I smell pizza?"

"I ordered three kinds—pepperoni for Reva, Canadian bacon and pineapple for me and Capri, and..." She pointed to a box with the lid still closed. "...sausage and black olives for you."

"Did you remember to add jalapenos?" she asked.

Lila nodded. "Of course."

Suddenly, Charlie Grace felt uneasy about broaching the subject pounding in her mind. Instead, she glanced around. "Did you paint?"

Her friend nodded a second time. "I was tired of that boring off-white. I had Camille help me, and we tackled the job on Monday night."

"In one night?" Reva asked, with arched eyebrows. She passed out paper plates and napkins.

"It wasn't hard. The worst part was moving all the furniture. Like I said, Camille helped. She pitched a fit about it, but I over-rode her objections by promising to take her shopping for a pair of designer jeans in payment."

Charlie Grace plopped down on the sofa next to Capri. "Ah, bribery. Works every time."

Lila went to the fridge and retrieved cans of beer and soda. She handed them off to her girlfriends. "Your turn is coming, Charlie Grace. Jewel will be in high school before you know it."

She shuddered. "Oh, don't say that."

Reva laughed. "Well, no matter what it cost you in time, effort, and bribery...this room is lovely."

Lila popped the top on her beer can. "You think so? I don't have a decorating bone in my body. I found a picture on Pinterest and just tried to duplicate it." She pointed to the sofa table. "Right down to those lamps. Found them on Amazon."

"I love online shopping," Capri said. "I only wish the retailers delivered overnight, like elsewhere in America."

"We're remote and in the boondocks," Reva said, grinning. "But a central pickup spot in town is better than nothing."

"Says the mayor, who only has to walk a half block to the post office to retrieve her deliveries," Lila teased.

Reva lifted her leg showing off her new Louboutins. "Carrying packages ain't easy while wearing stilettos, girls."

"Oh, my goodness, look at those!" Capri leaned for a better vantage spot. "When did you get those shoes?"

"Last week," Reva replied. She told them how she'd ruffled through dozens of online catalogs before she spotted the perfect pair and immediately ordered them with expedited shipping. "It was how I rewarded myself for helping with that ugly divorce case." She held up her hand. "No details. Attorney-client privilege. Girls, let me tell you—some people aren't the sort to give in to anything when they're angry, no matter how reasonable the request." She admired her shoes again. "Given that circus, I deserve these."

Capri pointed her thumb at Charlie Grace. "And then there are those who let their ex-husbands off the hook with barely an argument." She faked a cough. "No names mentioned."

"I did not let Gibbs off easy," Charlie Grace protested. "You can't get blood out of a turnip. Besides, he's Jewel's daddy. I didn't want World War III with the man who babysits on Friday nights so I can eat pizza and drink beer with my girlfriends. That alone is enough to stay friends, don't you think?"

Reva slid a slice of pizza onto her paper plate. "Yup, now tell us what you are hiding behind that innocent look on your face. I could see when you walked in the door that you had something on your mind." She took a bite. "Spill," she said, chewing.

Charlie Grace felt the heat of their stares. Suddenly, she considered her news too private to say out loud. How could she admit she had feelings for a guy who was nearly a stranger? Especially when she was securely fastened to Jason and had

been for a couple of years now. What did that even say
about her?

Lila pressed her hand on her arm. "Who can you tell if not
your best friends?"

Charlie Grace swallowed. "Well, it's like this..." She rubbed
her fingers across the side of her cheek. "I think I like a guy!"

Her three girlfriends exchanged shocked glances. "What?"
they shouted, nearly in unison.

Their questions tumbled over one another as their need for
information pummeled her.

"Who?" Reva demanded.

"I know who," Capri said. "McDreamy. From the bar."

"Who?" Reva repeated.

"What about Jason?" Lila inserted, taking the sensible
route. "You're already dating someone."

"I know that!" Charlie Grace moaned. "None of this makes
sense."

Reva tossed the remainder of her pizza slice onto the paper
plate in front of her. "But?"

"But, I..."

"Just start from the beginning," Capri urged. "Okay, we
know there was some attraction at the bar. We saw it, didn't we,
girls?" She looked to the others to confirm her statement.
When they nodded, she continued. "And we know he's staying
out at Teton Trails."

"So, what happened?" Reva said, interrupting. "Don't leave
anything out."

Charlie Grace lifted a beer from the table and popped the
top. "None of this goes any further."

Like when they were girls in high school, each of the
women crossed their hearts in a motion that promised secrecy.

"Now spill," Reva said. "The suspense is killing me."

Charlie Grace knew it would be difficult to convey everything just as it had happened, especially the way he made her

feel. Even saying what she'd been thinking constantly since their night by the campfire seemed surreal. At times, she'd convinced herself she had imagined it all. Yet, all she had to do was close her eyes and there he was...looking at her. Everything came rushing back.

"Okay, I admit I was a little bit attracted to Nick that night at the bar," she admitted.

"Nick? That's his name?" Lila asked.

"Nick Thatcher." Charlie Grace told them about his background in Los Angeles and his passion for photography. "I've never met anyone who loves a camera like that man." She recited everything she remembered about the early morning he had invited her to the river's edge and how they'd taken photographs of the moose and her baby.

"Something happened inside of me that I can't even explain," Charlie Grace told them. "It's as if my insides had taken a long nap and the time with Nick woke up feelings I'd forgotten how to experience."

"Feelings?" Capri prompted.

"Yearnings. Dissatisfaction with the status quo." She waved off her clouded explanation. "I don't know. It's hard to explain."

Reva tapped her long, painted fingernail against the coffee table. "Sounds like you're falling for him to me."

"No, it's not that exactly." Charlie Grace wasn't ready to admit what was going on inside her. She fidgeted nervously, her gaze fixated on her hands, trying to find the right words to convey the inexplicable whirlwind of emotions within her. Deep down, she knew Reva may be right, but admitting the fact felt like an admission of vulnerability. How could she explain the flutter in her chest whenever he was near, the way her heart skipped a beat at the sound of his voice?

She struggled to articulate the enchantment that enveloped her being, fearing that her girlfriends might see through her carefully constructed façade. She yearned for their understanding and support, yet the words remained trapped within her, tangled in a web of uncertainty. Was she even ready to confront the truth?

With a comforting touch on her hand, Reva looked her in the eyes. "Charlie Grace, love has a language of its own. Sometimes, love is meant to be felt before it can be fully understood. It's okay to be uncertain and hesitant; it's part of the journey. Trust your heart. It knows what it feels, even if your words struggle to catch up."

"Yeah, and we'll all be here, ready to listen and support you every step of the way," Lila added.

The wise words washed over her, easing her worries and kindling a glimmer of hope. In that moment, she realized she didn't need perfect eloquence. These women understood the language of her heart, even when she couldn't find the words to express it.

"But, what do I do about Jason?" she asked. "The last thing I want is to act like Gibbs and play fast and loose with someone's feelings. I'm not a female philanderer."

"Honesty is good," Reva offered.

"Yeah, and besides...it's time you move on. We all know your relationship with Jason isn't going anywhere. You're just not that into him."

Charlie Grace reached for her beer. "I don't want to hurt him. No doubt he's going to feel dumped."

Reva wagged her finger. "Girl, you aren't responsible for everyone's happiness."

"He's a big boy," Lila added. "It's more cruel to continue to lead him on. You need to get out of that relationship."

Charlie Grace took a deep breath. They were right, of course.

She knew deep down that it was time to let go, to release herself from the chains of complacency. But doubt gnawed at her, whispering false promises of familiarity and comfort.

With a trembling resolve, she mustered the strength to confront the inevitable truth. It was time to untangle herself from her stagnant relationship with Jason, to embrace the uncertainty that awaited her.

If she was with the wrong man...she was alone anyway.

Charlie Grace closed her eyes, took a deep breath, and repeated the mantra playing in her mind out loud. "I deserve more. I deserve to find a love that ignites my soul and propels me forward. It's time to let go of Jason and embark on a new path, even if it means walking away from what's comfortable."

And, at that moment, amidst the echoes of doubt and the concurrence of her girlfriends, she found the courage to break free and reclaim her own happiness.

24

R eva hated being late. To anything. Yet, here she was slipping into the AA meeting nearly twenty minutes after it started.

A number of town residents had stormed her office just as she was leaving. Apparently, the electricity in the town square wasn't working. With the annual oyster fry planned for tomorrow night, the issue couldn't wait.

When Brewster Findley, their local electrician, admitted the problem was beyond his capability, a company from Jackson was willing to send someone right out. What was initially thought to be defective wiring installed by Brewster turned out to simply be a rodent problem. Apparently, mice liked to chew on plastic.

By tomorrow night, the problem would be resolved. Emergency diverted.

Reva quietly slipped into a plastic chair at the back of the room and turned her attention to the front where Capri's stepfather had stepped to the podium.

The tension in the air was palpable as Dick Jacobs clutched

a piece of paper, his hands trembling. He took a deep breath, preparing himself to share. "Cancer is for the birds," he began.

His voice, filled with a mixture of sorrow and determination, resonated through the room as he unveiled the news of his recent cancer finding. Waves of shock and sympathy rippled across the faces of his fellow AA members, their expressions reflecting a deep understanding of the weight of such a diagnosis.

As Dick revealed his future, that he may only have months to live, Dot Montgomery dug inside her bag and fished out a used tissue. She blotted at the corners of her eyes and sniffled loudly.

Despite the raw emotion, the room became a sanctuary, a space where Dick could lay bare the struggles that accompanied his new journey. "Emily and Capri have been supportive. As have some of you in this room." His eyes met Reva's. "Family isn't always a matter of blood."

As he shared his journey and the unknown future he faced, the rawness of his fear and the uncertainty that now clouded his future became painfully evident.

One of the fundamental teachings in AA was acknowledging that individuals with addiction struggle with the illusion of control. Reva knew that everyone seated struggled to admit that powerlessness and surrender to a higher power. By letting go of the belief that they had control over life, their proclivity to use alcohol and other substance abuse diminished.

Sometimes that resolve was severely tested.

"I guess this is where the serenity thing takes over," Dick offered. "Funny thing. I've never been more scared....or more at peace, than I am right now."

When Dick finished and made his way back to his seat, the people in the room clamored to offer their friend solace and empathy. There were lots of hugs and pats on his back as their unwavering presence reminded him that he was not alone.

Reva sat quietly among the fellow members at the AA meeting, her gaze fixed on Dick as he wiped his face with his sleeved arm. The weight of his words lingered heavily in her heart, triggering a swirl of emotions within her.

Or, maybe it was Charlie Grace's recent news of her new relationship. Despite the complications, Reva was jealous of what might be on the horizon for her girlfriend.

It was in these moments that Reva realized once again the impact of losing Merritt, the hole the loss of that relationship had left.

Despite the deep bond she shared with her girlfriends, there was an ache, an unfulfilled longing that lingered in the depths of her being. Charlie Grace, Lila, and Capri were her confidantes, her pillars of support, but there was a void that their companionship couldn't quite fill.

Reva had never found the courage to admit this to anyone, but she yearned for something more—a mate, a partner who could unravel the complexities of her soul with a single glance. Someone who could understand the unspoken words that lingered between the lines of her laughter and wipe away the tears that fell in those moments of vulnerability.

As she watched couples strolling hand in hand, a pang of longing intensified. She craved a connection that transcended friendship, an intimate bond that only a mate could provide. While her girlfriends offered unwavering love, Reva knew deep down that her heart longed for a different kind of love—one that ignited passion, kindled romance, and promised a lifetime of shared dreams.

Seven years without Merritt.

She hadn't expected how lonely she would be without him.

25

Nestled in the center of the town square, a rustic mountain wood gazebo stood decorated with a colorful banner announcing the commencement of Thunder Mountain's annual Rocky Mountain Oyster Festival. People of all ages gathered, their faces beaming with excitement, ready to partake in the planned activities. Laughter and cheerful chatter resonated through the crowd, mingling with the lively tunes of a local band as the aroma of popcorn, cotton candy, and frying meat wafted in the air.

Charlie Grace held Jewel's hand as they walked briskly by Jason's side.

"Mommy, do I have to eat Rocky Mountain oysters? I don't like 'em."

"I'll eat yours," Jason heartily exclaimed. "They're delicious!"

She noticed Reva engaged in conversation with a cluster of individuals and eagerly waved in her direction.

Jason stretched his neck, craning to get a better view of the crowd. "Impressive turnout," he remarked, gesturing towards the gathering. "It appears Reva has donned her mayoral persona today, engaging with her constituents, particularly those of substantial means."

The comment immediately irked Charlie Grace. "Oh, I don't think that's true. Reva has plenty of money. Besides, she never wanted the mayor job. The townspeople begged her to step in and take over after Hank Peters passed."

"Yeah, I suppose you're right," Jason said, taking her hand. "Regardless, she does a good job." He gave Reva a wave.

Charlie Grace sighed. She couldn't remember a time when Jason had ever ventured to argue with her or express an opposing position. He always seemed to go along to get along.

Some women would appreciate that. She couldn't help but feel his passive nature was...well, uninspired and a little boring.

"You hungry?" he asked.

"Not especially, but I could eat."

"Well, I'm not eating any of those nasty things," Jewel announced.

"We heard you the first time," she reminded her daughter.

Jason reached in his back pocket, pulled out his wallet, and handed Jewel a dollar bill. "Bet you'll eat some of that cotton candy."

She beamed. "You bet! I love cotton candy. Especially the pink kind."

"What do you say?" Charlie Grace reminded.

"Oh, yeah." Her little girl looked up. "Thank you."

Charlie Grace granted Jason a weak smile, feeling her insides weaken as she considered what was ahead. After wrestling with the notion, she'd decided her girlfriends were right. Her relationship with Jason had run its course. She could no longer lead him to believe they had a future together. Jason was a nice man, so kind and generous. He was so sweet to Jewel, and so was his mother, Oma. But there was absolutely no spark.

While she wasn't one to make critical decisions based on simple emotions, she was now convinced there should be more.

She should feel something when she saw his name on her phone, or when he reached for her hand. A goodnight kiss on her doorstep should bring tingles to her toes, instead of a suppressed yawn.

Her dating relationship with Jason had come to an end. The hard part would be breaking the news to him.

She'd arranged for Aunt Mo to take Jewel home with her, providing for time alone with Jason when he drove her home tonight. She'd break her decision to him then.

"There's Daddy!" Jewel pulled her hand from her mother's grasp. "Can I go to him?"

Charlie Grace nodded. "Okay, but stay close. No taking off."

"I know."

Jason waved to a group of guys who were lined up at the fryers, paper plates in hand. "You hungry, now?" Jason asked, his eyes hopeful.

"Not really, but go ahead."

Jason nodded. "You sure? Because I can wait for you."

"No, you go on," she assured him. "I'll grab something to drink."

Charlie Grace headed for the large white tent filled with white tables and folding chairs.

Inside, Capri spotted her and hurried over. "Hey, Charlie Grace. Have you seen Reva or Lila yet?"

She shook her head. "Reva is here. But I haven't seen Lila. I'm sure she'll show up soon."

Capri stepped back and visually inspected Charlie Grace's outfit. "Is that new?"

She glanced down at her pink floral sundress. "This? No, I just haven't worn it in a while."

Her friend nodded with approval. "Well, it's cute. I don't see you wear dresses often. Is there an occasion?" She winked.

"No reason." Charlie Grace turned for the long table where

the members of the city council were pouring homemade root beer into frosted mugs.

Capri trailed behind her. "I'm just saying...if you wore that dress for someone special, it'll do the trick."

Charlie Grace made a point of ignoring the comment as Sam Cook offered her a mug, then handed another to Capri.

"Thanks, Sam," they said in unison as they placed some money into the donation can.

Capri leaned over and lowered her voice. "Don't look now, but your new friend is heading this way. From the way he's looking at you, I was right. He approves of the sundress."

Charlie Grace couldn't help it. Her heart skipped a beat. She took a deep breath and directed her attention to where Capri was not so subtly tilting her head.

"Hey." Nick smiled as he neared. "This is quite the affair."

Charlie Grace took in the man standing before her.

Nick's dark-washed jeans hugged his frame just right, accentuating his tall height. The fabric of his button-down shirt draped effortlessly against his torso, hinting at a toned physique. The rolled-up sleeves revealed a glimpse of sinewy forearms.

Charlie Grace had to steel herself to keep from staring. The feat was nearly impossible to achieve.

Capri elbowed her, smiling. "Who's your friend?"

The comment jerked Charlie Grace from her mental reverie. "Oh, sorry. Nick, this is one of my closest friends, Capri Jacobs." She turned to Capri. "This is Nick. He's a guest out at Teton Trails and the production designer for the television show *Bear Country* being filmed over on the outskirts of Jackson." She realized Capri knew most of this already, but her nerves seemed to be getting the best of her.

Capri smiled and extended her hand. "While we didn't formally meet, I think I saw you down at the Rustic Pine a few weeks back."

Recognition dawned on Nick's face. "Oh, yeah. I remember. You were there with Charlie Grace and some other women."

She nodded. "Girls' night out."

Nick rubbed the side of his chin while surveying the scene. "I'm intrigued with the idea that a remote town in Wyoming hosts an annual oyster fry. What? Do you have them flown in from Oregon?"

"Uh, no." Charlie Grace glanced over at Capri. "I think we've got us an oyster virgin," she said, grinning.

"Well, there's a cure for that!" came Capri's reply.

The women each looped arms with Nick and pulled him in the direction of the tables now loaded with hot oysters freshly pulled from the fryers. Capri grabbed a paper plate from a stack at the end of the table. Charlie Grace scooped several golden crisp oysters onto the plate and handed Nick a plastic fork. "Eat up!"

He glanced between them, puzzled.

One of the guys standing at the fryer let out a laugh that sounded a lot like a coyote howl. "A virgin?"

"Yup, but not for long," Charlie Grace told him.

Nick's face instantly grew skeptical. "Okay, something tells me everything is not on the up and up here."

Charlie Grace relented. "Okay, truth? These are Rocky Mountain Oysters. They're not exactly grown in the sea."

The old man at the fryer let out another howl. "Nope. These are bull oysters. Or, should I say they're from former bulls?" He winked at the girls.

"I'm not sure I understand what…"

"They're testicles," announced Lila, who came up from behind them.

Nick nearly dropped his plate. "Testicles?"

Lila nodded. "Yeah, when the bull calves are castrated, we save them and fry them up."

"Hence, the Rocky Mountain Oyster Festival," Capri announced.

Charlie Grace plucked one of the fried oysters from off his plate with her fingers and popped it in her mouth. While chewing, she reached for another. "They're delicious."

"They're yucky!" Jewel repeated, as she and her dad approached.

Gibbs reached for an oyster off Nick's plate and tossed it in his mouth. "Not true, puddin'. Not true."

"Try one," Charlie Grace urged.

Nick glanced between all the faces filled with the anticipation of watching him do the deed. He shrugged and glanced down at Jewel. "What the heck."

She scrunched her face. "You'll be sorry."

He gingerly placed an oyster inside his mouth, closed his eyes, and chewed. They all watched and waited.

Finally, he opened his eyes. "Not bad," he said and reached for another. "Not bad at all."

"C'mon. Admit it. They're really good," Charlie Grace said, motioning for the plate to be refilled.

She looked over at Nick and their eyes met. He had the deepest blue eyes of any man she'd ever seen.

"Hey, there you are."

Charlie Grace looked up to see Jason had returned. "I've been looking everywhere for you," he said, wearing a wide grin as he took her hand. "I have a surprise."

"A surprise?"

"Yeah, follow me." He led her through the crowd, past Oma, who winked as they passed. She followed as he climbed the steps to the gazebo. When he motioned to the band members, they immediately stopped the country tune they were playing and broke into the romantic ballad "Through the Years" made popular by Kenny Rogers.

Jason stepped to the microphone and cleared his throat. "Everyone, could I have your attention."

Charlie Grace's eyes widened as she watched a crowd gather, all eyes on them.

Jason dug in his pocket and plucked out a little black box. Before Charlie Grace could grasp what was going on, he dropped to one knee.

Charlie Grace couldn't breathe. "Jason, what are you doing...?" she whispered.

Before she could protest further, he looked up at her. "I'm not so good at things like this, but I wanted to make this special...so I'm doing it in front of the whole town."

Charlie Grace's eyes filled with tears. Not of joy, but of sheer panic.

As the crowd grew hushed, Jason, trembling with nervous energy, plucked a ring from the small velvet box in his hands. Gasps of delight filled the air as everyone, including Charlie Grace, realized what was about to happen.

"*No, Jason. No!*" she mentally screamed.

No amount of opposition could stop what was happening.

Jason fixed his gaze upon her face. "Charlie Grace...will you marry me?"

26

"He proposed at an oyster fry? How romantic!" Capri's voice dripped with sarcasm. She leaned against the sink in the public restroom. "I mean, you don't see many country songs written about that."

"Stop! This isn't funny!" Charlie Grace protested. "What am I going to do?"

Reva parked her hands on her hips. "You're going to stop and make this right. You can't marry Jason. We won't let you."

Lila pulled the straw cowboy hat from her head and straightened her hair before putting it back in place. "Why in the world did you take that ring in the first place? I mean, you aren't going to marry him."

Charlie Grace groaned. "What was I supposed to do? Humiliate him in front of all those people? Did any of you miss the fact that the whole town was watching, including Oma?"

"Dumb move on his part, if you ask me." Capri turned to the mirror and checked her hair. "How did he know you'd say yes in the first place? That little stunt was a risk he chose to take."

The locked door rattled.

"Just a minute," Reva called out. She turned to her stricken friend. "Charlie Grace, I'm not sure what got into you up there, but you've got to get with Jason and correct this immediately. A match has been lit and this entire thing will blow up into a wildfire if you don't put it out immediately."

The door rattled again.

"Just a minute!" they all called out.

Charlie Grace's eyes filled with tears. "It was Oma. His mother's face was filled with such an expression of happiness. The most joy I've ever seen from the dear woman, and that's saying a lot. And Jason, I mean...I—what was I supposed to say with him holding my hand and looking at me like that?" She sniffed and searched for a tissue. "I couldn't even think!"

Lila crammed a wad of toilet paper into Charlie Grace's hand. She wasn't normally a crier, but this had her completely undone.

"Oh, for goodness' sake!" Capri parked her hands on her hips. "You have got to stop trying to please everyone. Your happiness counts as much, if not more, than anyone's. Put yourself first, for once."

Reva held up her hands. "Okay, we're getting nowhere chastising Charlie Grace for what she said up there. Right now, she needs our support." She took both of Charlie Grace's hands in hers. "What do you need, Charlie Grace? We're here for you."

She looked up miserably. "Turn the clock back and make it all go away." Her lip quivered. "Did anyone see where Nick went?" She fought to keep from wailing. "Oh, goodness! What he must think!"

Reva pulled Charlie Grace into a reassuring hug. "You can fix this."

"You've got to fix this," Lila added. "I mean, really, Charlie Grace. You can't marry Jason."

Charlie Grace drew a deep breath. They were right. She had to undo what had been done. The sooner, the better. No doubt everyone out there was chattering about the surprise engagement and upcoming nuptials. Oma and her Knit Wits group were likely already organizing the reception dinner. Betty Dunning would plan to make her signature homemade mints and Dorothy Vaughn would be intent on stocking up on pineapple juice, orange sherbet, and 7-Up for her punch.

The thought made Charlie Grace feel nauseous.

Then it hit her. Jewel was in the crowd. She had to get this cleared up and break the news to her daughter that there was no wedding on the horizon. At least no wedding to Jason Griffith.

How could she let this happen? It was as if she'd had an out-of-body experience. Jason slipped that ring on her finger and everything that followed was a blur.

Determined, she grabbed a paper towel from the dispenser and ran it under a blast of cold water. She patted her face, relishing the cool feel against the heat of the moment.

There was no escaping what she'd done—or failed to do—but there was no holding back now. Not if she didn't want to be Mrs. Jason Griffith.

Charlie Grace tossed the damp paper towel in the trash receptacle and turned to face her benefactors. "Okay, I'm ready," she announced. "I have to fix this."

THANKFULLY, Charlie Grace's girlfriends had her back. They followed her from the restroom as determined as she was to clear the situation.

Lila nodded to the impatient woman who waited outside the door. "All yours."

Reva made a beeline for Gibbs and Jewel, promising to take them aside and alert them as to the situation. No doubt, Gibbs would relentlessly tease her about this for months to come.

She'd just have to deal with it. There was no erasing what she'd done up on that gazebo. She simply had to move forward and correct her mistake. Take the knocks as they came.

Jewel and Lila would go on the hunt for Nick. While they would refrain from any detailed explanation, they assured Charlie Grace they would tell him to wait and hold off on drawing any conclusions from the event that had just occurred, and that she would not be marrying Jason. She'd see him back at the ranch and they'd talk.

The rest of those who had witnessed her faux pas would learn of the reversal soon enough. Gossip flew in this town. All they'd have to do is clue in Nicola Cavendish and she'd broadcast the news far and wide. Like anything of this nature, there would be lots of chatter. Eventually, people would tire of talking of Charlie Grace's misfortune, and it would die down, only to be brought up occasionally at pinochle club or sadly, bible study—all in the ruse of praying for the situation and the parties involved.

Charlie Grace took a deep breath. After looking back at her girlfriends for mental fortitude, she marched toward Jason.

"Hey, honey." Emboldened by the fact they were now engaged, he pulled her into a tight embrace. In a move he'd never ventured earlier, he reached and patted her bottom, then looked at her, beaming.

"We need to talk...now."

"Sure, sweetheart. What's up?"

She grabbed his forearm and pulled him toward the parking area and to an unoccupied park bench.

Once seated, she tried to find the right words. Despite her resolve, her insides trembled. "Listen, Jason..."

He grabbed her hand and brought it to his lips. "Anything you need or want—you've got it."

Charlie Grace could barely breathe.

As the sun dipped below the horizon, casting a soft glow

over the silhouetted buildings of Thunder Mountain, Charlie Grace took a deep breath, summoning every ounce of courage within her. These years together had woven a tapestry of memories, yet the truth lingered heavily in her heart.

With tears welling in her eyes, she turned to Jason. "I can't marry you," she whispered, her voice trembling with vulnerability.

His brow furrowed, confusion etching lines across his face.

Charlie Grace went on, her voice barely audible. "As much as I'd like it to be different, I can't do this. I can't marry you, Jason."

"Why?" His voice cracked. "We've been together for years."

"I know," she nodded. "But, I've realized that I don't love you in the way you deserve to be loved. It wouldn't be fair to either of us to spend a lifetime pretending otherwise."

An agonizing silence settled between them, filled only by the faint rustling of the leaves on the nearby aspen tree. The weight of her words hung in the air, forever altering their path together.

A stunned hush enveloped the man on the bench beside her, as if the world had momentarily frozen around him. Jason's gaze ventured up and met Charlie Grace's, searching for any sign of hesitation or doubt. "You said yes," he whispered.

"I know. I'm sorry."

His voice, though laced with anguish, remained remarkably composed. "But...all these years," he began, his words wavering with a mix of confusion and heartbreak. "I thought...I believed that we were building something real, something lasting." His eyes welled up, mirroring the pain in Charlie Grace's eyes. "I love you. I thought you felt the same way."

His voice quivered, aching with unspoken questions. "What changed? Was it me? Was it something I did or didn't do?" A fragile vulnerability emerged, his heart laid bare before her, longing for answers that might mend the pieces of his shattered heart.

At that moment, Charlie Grace hated herself. Jason did not deserve this.

She reached out, her hand shaking as she touched his. Her voice, filled with regret and raw honesty, answered his silent questions. "It's not you," she whispered, her voice choked with emotion. "You've been only good to me and to Jewel. You're a genuinely sweet man, and I was most certainly drawn to that right from the start." She swallowed. "I can't control the way my heart feels. The love I've been searching for...it's not there when I'm with you."

There, she'd addressed the central issue head-on. Something of this magnitude could hardly be softened. What could she possibly say that would make the final message any easier? Still, the look on his face nearly crushed her.

"I still don't understand. Why did you take the ring if you had no intention of marrying me?"

"I—well, I got caught up in the moment. I mean, you surprised me. I was off guard and...well, Jason. I'm so very sorry. Never did I mean to hurt you in any way." She dared to look him in the face. "No matter how much I want this story to play out the way you'd hoped, I don't love you."

He ran his hand through the top of his hair. The motion left a strand sticking up. "I...we've dated for a long time. I thought—"

"I don't want to hold you back from finding the kind of love that consumes your soul, the love that lights up your eyes. You deserve that and so much more."

Jason's face became a canvas of sorrow. He drew a shuddering breath, his fingers gripping hers tightly. "Maybe, given time, you'll change your mind?"

Charlie Grace shook her head. "No."

She took that moment to return the ring and tucked it inside his palm with a kiss to his cheek.

He leaned against the back of the park bench in defeat. "I won't pretend this doesn't hurt, that it won't take time to heal," he admitted, his voice quivering. "But if you're sure, truly sure this is what you want, then I won't stand in your way."

A bittersweet silence fell over them as they sat, their intertwined hands a testament to the friendship they'd shared for so long. In that moment, they both understood that even though their paths had diverged, friendship would continue and remain imprinted on both their hearts.

27

C harlie Grace pulled the ranch pickup into the yard and cut the engine. She sat quietly for several seconds, noting that the lights were off in the main house, an indication that Aunt Mo had gotten her daughter home and safely in bed. Her father too.

No doubt Charlie Grace would have a lot to explain at breakfast.

Her eyes went to Nick's cabin as it came into view, her spirits lifting slightly when she saw it lit up.

Slipping out of the truck, Charlie Grace closed the door softly, her footsteps barely audible on the gravel path as she made her way toward the cabin. Drawing closer, she caught sight of Nick standing on the porch, waiting for her.

"Hey..." he said, as she neared.

The events of the entire evening flickered across Charlie Grace's mind, resembling a bad movie she wished she hadn't played a starring role in.

"I'm glad to see you," she said as she climbed a couple of wooden steps up to the porch. "Thanks for waiting up."

"I hate to admit it," Nick began, a slight grin tugging at the corners of his mouth. "But that was some top-notch drama. I mean, don't get me wrong. When he slipped that ring on your finger, my heart plummeted to the floor. But, wow..." He ran his hands through his hair and shook his head.

Charlie Grace buried her face in her hands. "I'm mortified. I have no idea why I didn't refuse that ring. Marrying Jason was never my intention."

Nick gently reached out, intertwining his fingers with hers. "You got swept up in the story," he offered.

She nodded miserably. "I suppose. But, goodness...that was a train wreck. I'm so ashamed I let it happen."

"Ah, don't be. Life gets messy."

He guided her to a seat beside him. "Do you want to talk about it?"

She gave him a sheepish grin. "Honestly? Not really. But I do owe you an explanation."

"You owe me nothing," he insisted.

Leaning back, Charlie Grace gazed into the night sky, a tapestry of shimmering stars that seemed infinitely vast compared to her dim situation. Everything seemed big compared to how small she felt right now. "It's over between me and Jason," she told him. "I had planned to end things tonight, before...well, before everything exploded into the worst moment of my entire life."

"Worst moment ever?" Nick echoed, raising an eyebrow.

In the distance, a frog's methodic honking could be heard over a chorus of insects.

"Okay, perhaps I'm exaggerating a bit. I've had my fair share of worse moments," she admitted, stealing a glance at him before letting a mischievous grin blossom across her face. "But you have to admit, that was a classic bombshell."

Returning her grin, Nick leaned back in his chair, his gaze drifting upward. "True, it was pretty spectacular."

A surge of feather-like light flooded through Charlie Grace

at the shared humor, dispelling the heaviness that had plagued her since the gazebo fiasco. "The silver lining is that I'm free now. If there were someone else I had my eye on, I could pursue that relationship without any guilt." She turned to face him directly. "And, well, there is someone else."

"Oh?" Nick responded, his interest clearly piqued.

"Yeah, he's a hotshot from L.A., a production designer with a passion for wildlife photography. Oh, and he has an undeniable weakness for rib eye steaks and Rocky Mountain oysters."

"I'm already liking this guy," Nick teased, a sparkle in his eyes.

Charlie Grace turned fully towards him, a newly discovered joy suddenly radiating from her being. She pushed her earlier embarrassment aside and reached for his hand. "Me, too. I happen to like him a lot."

28

I n the flurry of events of the past days, Charlie Grace almost forgot that Lizzy Cayman was due in from Seattle. This morning, at the crack of dawn and before she could jump in the shower, Albie called reporting his niece had safely arrived from Seattle. He planned to drive her out to Teton Trails when he shut the newspaper office down for lunch.

True to his word, the dusty yellow Volkswagen van rumbled up the gravel driveway a few minutes past noon.

After parking, Albie climbed out, beaming. He hurried around the van and opened the passenger door. Charlie Grace couldn't make out the conversation as he invited his niece out of his vehicle, but Albie seemed excited as he pointed toward the barn, the main lodge, and finally in her direction. She gave them both a welcoming wave before making her way to greet them.

The pretty young woman wore white jeans and a blue peasant-style top that showed off her bare shoulders. Charlie Grace would kill to have her thick, deep brown hair. "Welcome to the ranch, Lizzy." She extended her hand. "I'm Charlie Grace, the owner."

Lizzy gave a half-hearted nod and scanned the ranch with a raised eyebrow. "So, this is it, huh?" She shook her head. "It's sure not Seattle."

Charlie Grace nodded, undaunted by Lizzy's skeptical expression. "It's a different kind of beauty out here, but I assure you, the mountain air grows on you. I think you're going to enjoy working with us here at Teton Trails. We're a small, but close-knit team, striving to give our guests an unforgettable experience. You'll be helping with making up the cabins and assisting my aunt Mo with meal prep."

Lizzy turned to her uncle. "You said I'd be doing something more...challenging. Law school student here, remember?"

Albie didn't seem fazed by his niece's rudeness. He continued to beam as he placed his arm around her shoulders. "You're going to love working with Charlie Grace and Mo. You can't find nicer people anywhere."

Likewise, Charlie Grace maintained her calm demeanor, despite the growing realization that Lizzy might prove to be a handful. "Well, Lizzy, I'm certain a break from the rigor of legal research might just be the ticket. Making beds might not be glamorous, but this job comes with a lot of rewards."

"Yeah? Like?"

"A paycheck." Without waiting for a response, Charlie Grace turned and headed for the main lodge. Several steps down the path, she turned to see Lizzy gaping. "Well, are you coming?"

Albie urged his niece forward, and they followed Charlie Grace.

"You'll be expected to show up promptly at six o'clock am. You should be done by early afternoon each day," Charlie Grace told her new employee after showing her around. "If you do a good job and make it to the end of summer without quitting, there will be a cash bonus."

Despite the carrot she'd just dangled, it was her bet that this spoiled brat wouldn't last until the end of the week.

She was wrong.

Despite the shaky introduction, Lizzy turned out to be a hard worker. Rarely did Charlie Grace need to tell her anything twice. She seemed to work particularly well with Aunt Mo and never complained about the early hours or the tubs of potatoes she was tasked with peeling every morning.

That didn't mean Lizzy was a model employee. Albie's niece did not go out of her way to take on anything not assigned to her. Rarely did she engage with any of the guests, nor did she smile much. But she completed everything Charlie Grace asked her to do and performed the tasks properly.

Her free time was spent in her cabin or driving Albie's Volkswagen around. A few days into her stay, her uncle made his way out to the ranch and handed her the keys. "I don't need it," he explained. "I walk everywhere I need to go."

The girl snatched the keys with barely a thank you, leading Charlie Grace's instincts to flash warning lights. She decided to check her concern with her trusted aunt, who was a good judge of character. "Aunt Mo, how do you think Lizzy is doing?"

The brief silence that followed was all Charlie Grace needed to confirm her reservations.

Her aunt stopped paring the apple in her hand. "Well," she slowly began. "I'm not one to say anything bad about anyone. So, let me just say this—peacocks are beautiful birds, but they like to flaunt their feathers."

Aunt Mo was spot on.

"Yes," Charlie Grace agreed. "Albie's niece is very...uh, self-confident." She didn't voice her bigger concern.

Peacocks were not friendly birds.

Worse, they were prone to attack if you dared turn your back.

That was exactly what Charlie Grace tried to explain to

Reva, Lila, and Capri on their Friday night meet-up at the Rustic Pine.

"Why did the girl ever agree to come to Thunder Mountain if she didn't want to be here?" Reva asked as she took a seat at their corner table. "I mean, surely there are plenty of summer jobs in Seattle."

Charlie Grace reached for her beer mug. "I don't have a good answer for that. I'm not sure the feeling is mutual, but it's clear that Albie adores her. Just between us, Albie slipped and said something the other night when he came out to the ranch to visit her that suggested he may be paying her college tuition."

Capri's mouth fell open. "Wow, that's generous."

"Maybe he's footing her education bill because she's his only niece and he wants to help his sister out?" Reva offered.

Lila lifted her beer from the table. "Well, if he's spreading that love around, I've got a daughter going to college soon. She brought home a stack of information from the guidance counselor's office the other day and it all reads like Greek. I mean —*FAFSA, Cost of Attendance, Expected Family Contribution, Grant, Loan, Merit Aid*—a person needs a translator for all that jargon. So, if Albie is handing out checks, I'll take one."

"Does Albie even have that kind of money?" Capri asked. "I mean, college is expensive."

Reva dug inside her designer bag for her credit card. "Albie is the gold standard of human beings. I'm not surprised at his generosity toward his niece." She placed her card on the table-top. "Besides, I think Albie has money."

The revelation that Albie might be wealthy caught Charlie Grace off guard. "Oh, how could that be?" she argued. "He's the editor of the town paper. Has been since I can remember. He lives in a very humble house, drives a vintage Volkswagen van. Have you seen his clothes? He still wears corduroys that haven't been in style since the seventies."

Reva shrugged. "He's frugal. That doesn't suggest his bank account isn't bulging."

"True," Charlie Grace admitted. She picked at the corner of her napkin and sighed. "I only hope that niece of his isn't taking advantage."

Lila stood and dug a quarter out of her jeans pocket. "Why do you say that?" Her friend stepped to the nearby jukebox and plugged in the coin. "How about some Jason Aldean?" she called over her shoulder.

Capri nodded. "Have you heard his new one? I love that song."

Charlie Grace listened to her friends' exchange while she pondered her answer for several seconds. Like Aunt Mo, she was reluctant to give voice to her worries and be publicly critical. Finally, she responded, "Oh, I don't know. Just a gut feeling that he's awfully fond of the girl and might not be alert to being used."

"He's not being used if he's willingly paying for her schooling," Reva reminded.

Charlie Grace smothered a groan and tried to smile. "True."

Reva covered Charlie Grace's hand with her own. "Besides, you have a lot on your plate to think about without taking on Albie's potential troubles."

Capri drained her beer mug. "Agreed. It's time you focus on yourself for a change." She turned to Charlie Grace. "So, how's McDreamy?"

Charlie Grace rolled her eyes. "Would you quit calling him that? And Nick is just fine." A shy smile nipped at the corners of her mouth. "More than fine really."

"Do tell." Reva urged.

"Well, despite me being swamped out at the ranch, we've spent a lot of time together. Mainly, we've been shooting photographs. I took him to Hayden Valley in Yellowstone just before dusk. We spotted a grizzly and two cubs on the hillside and got a few fabulous shots."

She pulled out her phone and opened her photo app. "I loaded them here so I could show you." She passed her phone to Reva.

"Those are amazing, Charlie Grace." Reva flipped the image to the next. "I hope you stayed at a safe distance."

Lila impatiently held out her hand. "Let me see."

Reva passed the phone over. Lila buried her attention in the photographs, flipping them until she reached one that particularly drew her interest. "Oh, Charlie Grace. This one of you... well, it's stunning."

Capri leaned over for a look. "Wow! That's a Jack and Rose moment. I mean, the most romantic scene of the entire *Titanic* movie was when Jack painted her naked."

Charlie Grace huffed in protest. "I was hardly naked."

Capri grinned. "Oh, but clothes—or lack of—isn't the issue. Nick captured your essence. He saw what few others see."

Charlie Grace picked up her phone and studied the picture. "And that would be?"

"Well, in my opinion, that photograph captures an elusive interplay of emotions, vulnerability, and strength...all at the same time. The image goes beyond the confines of the frame." Capri pointed to the camera in Charlie Grace's hand. "See the glimmer in your eyes, the hint of a smile gracing your lips, and the gentle curve of your posture? Nick put *you* on film."

"Ooh, he did!" Lila agreed. She waved as Pastor Pete approached the table.

Pete wiped his hands on a towel and passed out clean bar napkins that were imprinted with the words *Sip slowly, savor life's blessings.*

"Hey, girls! Nice to see you tonight. You ready for a second round?"

Reva pushed her credit card his way. "Yes, and this one's on me."

Pete nodded and picked up the card. "Coming right up."

Charlie Grace held up her hand. "Make mine a soda this time."

Pete grinned. "Sure thing."

As soon as he moved from the table, Lila leaned in. "So, spill. Tell us everything. Did he kiss you?"

Reva nodded in the direction of the door where Nicola Cavendish was entering the bar. "Shh...keep your voices down. Let's not invite trouble," she warned.

Lila repeated herself in a whisper. "Well? Did he?"

A small smile danced on her lips. "Maybe."

29

C harlie Grace rested her elbow on the open window of her pickup on her way home from the Rustic Pine. The cool night air carried the faint grape-like scent of lupine. Above, stars crowded the dark sky.

Time spent with Reva, Lila, and Capri always did her heart good. Their bond extended beyond just being friends. They were an integral part of each other's lives, always providing perspective and encouragement. None of her girlfriends were shy in pointing out ways she'd gone off course. Especially when it came to her love life.

She supposed she had them to thank, at least in part, for her new relationship with Nick. Without their prodding, she may never have found the courage to move on from Jason and open herself to this new possibility.

Of course, there remained obstacles. When it came to her happiness, there were always roadblocks, it seemed. It wasn't easy to juggle the needs of everyone she loved with her own. Her friends were right, too often she put herself last.

It felt good to focus on Nick and their relationship even if their time together would be short-lived. Eventually, he would return to Los Angeles. She'd accepted that. But she vowed to enjoy every moment while he was here.

Charlie Grace nervously twirled a strand of hair between her fingers as the night air drifted through the open car window.

She couldn't help but feel a magnetic pull towards Nick. There was something about the way he looked at her, as if he could see straight through the walls she had carefully built around her heart. It was both thrilling and terrifying, the vulnerability he effortlessly coaxed out of her. She had grown independent and guarded, but with Nick, she could finally let go and be herself without fear of judgment.

She stared at the road before her, smiling at the very thought of him, the way he looked at her—the way he made her *feel*.

A tingle formed in her stomach at the memory of when he'd kissed her.

Armed with their cameras, she and Nick had ventured into Yellowstone, driving over an hour in hopes of catching a glimpse of a grizzly.

"Our best bet is Hayden Valley," she told him. "Especially at dusk."

"Do you really think we'll spot some bears?"

She pointed to a large pull-out and motioned for him to stop. "Grizzly Overlook, near the north end of Hayden Valley, is likely the best spot." She pointed. "By walking up that hilltop, we'll be able to see both directions across the valley. If we don't see any here, the north end of the valley is also good, since the Wapiti Lake pack tends to be active near there."

Nick parked and they grabbed their camera gear and got out. Charlie Grace tucked a can of bear spray in her backpack, just in case.

Their steps were hushed as the mountain terrain cast long shadows that migrated across the broad expanse of grass and sagebrush straddled by the Yellowstone River. The banks were lined with bison taking an evening drink.

As they reached the crest of Grizzly Overlook, there they were—a mama bear and two adorable cubs frolicking in the meadow, a sight that never got old.

"There," she pointed. "See them?"

Nick's face turned excited. "Wow!" he silently mouthed, while scrambling to ready his camera.

Her fingers trembled slightly as she adjusted her camera settings, wanting to capture every intricate detail. Nick stood beside her, his eyes sparkling with excitement. Together, they silently snapped away, freezing moments of wild wonder in their frames.

Far too soon, the bears crested the hillside and were out of sight.

Charlie Grace's heart pounded like a herd of wild bison, as she watched Nick adjust the settings on his camera before tucking it inside its case. He turned to her with a warm smile that made her knees feel weak. "Charlie Grace, this has been an incredible experience. I couldn't have asked for a better guide and companion."

She felt a blush color her cheeks, and she laughed softly. "I'm glad you enjoyed it. I love sharing this with someone who appreciates the wilderness and all its wonder."

He reached for her hand, and they headed in the direction of his car. The sound of trickling water over rocks, as they strolled along the river, provided a backdrop to their conversation.

"Hey, I'm leaving on Saturday. I need to make a short trip back to Los Angeles for some business. I'd love it if you came with me."

She shook her head. "I can't. As much as I'd love to, my

obligations simply won't allow me to get away right now. I have Jewel, and the ranch, and..."

"I figured that might be the case. Can't say I'm not disappointed." He squeezed her hand as he stepped over a large lava rock. "Careful," he warned. "Don't trip."

"How long will you be gone?" She held her breath as she stepped over the rock, dreading the response.

"Not long," he told her. "Only a day or two."

His answer brought an immediate smile to her face.

"What?" he asked, looking at her as if she were the most important person on the planet.

"Nothing. I'm just glad it's a short trip."

"Because you'll miss me?" he teased.

"Yes," she admitted. "I'm going to miss you."

And she would miss him...terribly.

It was hard to express how tightly her heart had formed around the idea of Nick Thatcher in her life. He was the first thing she thought of when she woke. His face was the last image in her mind as she drifted to sleep. Every moment in between was filled with replays of every conversation, every look...every touch.

While thrilling, the feeling scared her—this intensity over him. Rushing into this kind of connection didn't feel safe. She was setting herself up for future hurt. Especially when he left her permanently.

Despite the fear, she couldn't help but move forward. It was as if there was some force drawing her closer and closer to a bright flame where she was bound to get burned eventually.

None of that mattered.

She didn't want to use better judgment. She didn't want to be sensible. She didn't want to give him up until she had to. The idea of life without Nick Thatcher strolling across the ranch lawn toward her seemed bland and tasteless. The only option was to enjoy every moment...now.

Charlie Grace glanced at Nick, who seemed lost in thought as well, and she wondered if he felt the same emotional stirrings she did—a notion quickly dispelled when he suddenly stopped and turned to face her.

As the last rays of sunlight bathed them in a warm glow, Charlie Grace's heart skipped a beat. There was a flicker of uncertainty in Nick's eyes, and she could tell he was grappling with something.

"Charlie Grace," he began, his voice soft and earnest, "I have to be honest with you. This time in Wyoming has been more than just a job and a photography adventure for me."

A surprising wave of need swept over her as she took a step closer to him. "What do you mean, Nick?"

He took a deep breath, his gaze never leaving hers. "I mean that being with you, spending time together...it's been completely unexpected. It feels like there's something special here, something beyond friendship."

Unexpected tears welled up in her eyes as she realized he was expressing the very emotions she'd been trying to contain. "I feel it too," she whispered. "This is unlike anything I've ever experienced."

He reached out and gently brushed a strand of hair away from her face, his touch sending shivers down her spine. "I don't want to rush into anything, but I can't deny how I am starting to feel about you, Charlie Grace." He paused. "I've circled the earth enough years to know it's rare to find this kind of connection."

Her heart soared, and she placed her hand over his, savoring the warmth of his touch. "I feel the same way. It's like I've found a missing piece of myself."

Nick leaned in, his breath mingling with hers, and their lips met in a tender, heartwarming kiss. It was a kiss filled with hope and the promise of something beautiful.

Now, as the pickup cruised down the highway, Charlie

Grace reached for the radio dial. She hummed along to the tune that played, remembering the way he tasted, the way he smelled, the way his hand felt on her back. Something told her that the kiss symbolized a threshold crossed.

There was no going back, and she didn't want to.

30

Reva parked her car in front of Dick Jacobs' house with a mix of concern and affection in her heart. Dick had been an important part of her AA journey, often offering quiet guidance and support, as she had for him. Learning about his cancer diagnosis left her with a heavy heart. Being there for him, as well as Capri and her mother, was the least she could do.

She grabbed her bag and the pie she'd purchased from the Heavenly Bites Bakery, then stepped from the car, taking care as she traversed the gravel driveway in her stilettos. Someday she'd accept that Thunder Mountain was no place for four-inch heels. Oh, but how she loved the way she looked in them!

She approached the door and knocked gently. Moments later, Capri's mother opened the door.

"Hi, Emily." Reva held the pie out. "This is for you and Dick."

The woman's eyes widened. "Oh, my. You didn't have to do that."

Reva leaned and gave Emily a quick hug. "I wanted to. It's

huckleberry. Leona told me she pulled it from the oven only an hour before I bought it."

"Well, it looks delicious. Come in." She ushered her inside.

The living room was like stepping back in time. An eclectic mix of vintage furnishings filled the space, including a plush, mustard-yellow velvet couch adorned with colorful paisley throw pillows. A sleek teakwood coffee table displayed well-worn copies of *Good Housekeeping* magazine and a couple of Louis L'Amour western novels. In the corner, a pile of vinyl records sat on the floor next to a record player.

"Would you like a cup of coffee?" Emily offered. "We can sample this pie."

Reva shook her head. "Not for me. Thanks." She glanced around the room. "I came to check on Dick. How is he?"

As if on cue, Dick appeared wearing a blue flannel shirt, baggy jeans, and slippers and looking more haggard than the last time she saw him. "Hey, Reva," Dick greeted warmly. "Thanks for coming by. Please, make yourself comfortable."

Reva took a seat on the couch as Dick settled into an armchair opposite her.

"How are you holding up?" Reva asked, concern evident in her voice.

Dick took a deep breath before answering. "It's been a whirlwind, to say the least. The diagnosis was a shock, but I'm trying to face it head-on."

Emily stood near and patted her husband's shoulder. "He has a great medical team in Cheyenne and has started treatment."

Reva had learned that much from Capri but wanted to know more about what lay ahead for her friend. "What's the plan?"

Emily didn't wait for Dick to answer. "Initially, the prognosis was grim. But we've learned there are options. He's scheduled for surgery next week. They'll be removing the tumor from his liver and surrounding lymph nodes. Then, depending on what they find, he might need some follow-up treatment, like radiation or chemotherapy."

Reva nodded, absorbing the information. "That sounds intense. But you're a strong person, Dick. I have faith that you'll pull through this."

It was a lie. She'd performed some internet research. The findings were not good. There was no promise Dick would make it out of this. Still, she believed in hope...and miracles. She certainly was praying for one.

"I hope so," Dick replied, a hint of vulnerability in his voice. "It's scary, you know? Facing the unknown, the uncertainty of it all. But, like Emily said, I've got a great medical team and support from family and friends, including you." He looked up at his wife and squeezed her hand. "Emily has been my rock."

Reva nodded in agreement. "You are not alone in this fight," she assured him. "We're all here for you, every step of the way."

"I know, and I'm grateful for that," Dick said, his eyes suddenly welling up with tears. "I haven't always been a good person. It's still hard to believe so many folks here in Thunder Mountain care about me."

"Of course, we do," Reva said gently. "It's okay to feel scared. Allow yourself to lean on us when you need to. What we learn in AA isn't only applicable to battling our demons with alcohol, the principles are universal and apply to life. Remember, strength is often found in our willingness to be vulnerable and honest."

Dick nodded, wiping away a tear. "Thank you, Reva. Your support means the world to me."

Driving away from her morning encounter, Reva made her way to her office, her mind filled with thoughts of Dick. His resilience in the face of his diagnosis left her feeling a profound admiration. The road ahead would be hard, especially for Emily and Capri. No doubt his diagnosis had served as a reminder of the fragility of life, prompting them to cherish every moment they had with him and to lean on each other for strength.

Reva entered her office in Thunder Mountain with purpose. She would be there for them, support those two women in every way possible in the coming months.

She'd been settled into her office chair less than ten minutes before her assistant appeared in the doorway, her silver hair neatly pinned in a bun and cat-eye glasses perched on the end of her nose.

Verna Billingsley was a character who seemed to have stepped out of a different era. Despite the world's technological advancements, Verna had managed to remain steadfastly disconnected from the digital age. Her desk was cluttered with stacks of paper, and she relied on an old-fashioned electric typewriter to compose her memos and letters. When it came to dealing with emails and spreadsheets, she looked at the computer screen on her boss's desk as if it were an alien object, unsure what to make of it.

Nevertheless, Verna's charm lay in her sincere dedication and unwavering loyalty to her job, and to Reva. Despite her aversion to modern technology, she somehow managed to keep the mayor's office and Reva's law practice both running like clockwork.

"Nicola Cavendish showed up a half hour ago demanding to see you," Verna announced. "I told her you were not due in for another hour. She said she'd be back."

Reva's heart sank. Nicola was not one to bring good news. "When she gets here, bring her on in."

Verna had not made it back to her desk when the front door opened and Reva heard Nicola's voice. "Well, is the mayor in yet? I hope she realizes she's on taxpayer dollars and there are constituents who expect her to be here."

The comment irked Reva. She was not bound to a set time

behind the mayor's desk and most certainly not obligated to be at Nicola Cavendish's beck and call. Still, Reva knew better than to react. She pasted a smile and went out to greet the woman.

Upon seeing Reva in the doorway, Nicola's face suddenly grew bright and cheery. "Well," she said, making a point of looking at her watch. "Good morning!"

Reva swallowed her disdain. "Good morning, Nicola. What can I do for you?"

Nicola set her red purse down on the armchair and lifted her chin. "Reva, we need to talk," she said, her tone suddenly dripping with condescension.

"Of course, Nicola. What's on your mind?" Reva maintained a calm exterior despite her building inner apprehension.

"I've called an emergency town meeting for this evening," Nicola announced. "And I expect you to be there."

Reva's eyebrows furrowed in confusion. "An emergency town meeting? What's the issue, Nicola?"

"You'll learn fully this evening," Nicola shot back. "But I'll tell you this much—it's about the proposed television production I spoke with you about earlier."

Reva's heart skipped a beat. She'd been carefully handling the situation, fielding the few voiced concerns raised by some of the townspeople, mostly while in the grocery store aisle or the bookstore. Mainly, there were questions—many of which she had no real answers for. And for the number of concerns, there appeared to be an equal number of people excited about what the production might mean for tourism.

"Nicola, I understand that the local television production is a sensitive topic, but there's no need to stir up trouble," Reva said firmly. "Calling an emergency meeting could create unnecessary tension. Especially without discussing it with me first."

"I brought my concerns to you, and you did nothing to alleviate the issue. I had no choice but to take matters into my own hands," Nicola retorted. "I won't have you dismissing the concerns of the people of this town."

Deeply angered by her accusations, Reva took a deep breath, trying to keep her composure. "I am not dismissing anyone's concerns, but I need to ensure we take all of the feelings of our townspeople into consideration and approach this issue thoughtfully and collaboratively. We can't afford to let emotions dictate our actions."

Nicola's eyes narrowed, and a calculating smile played on her lips. "Do I need to remind you of my husband's influence in this town...and mine? We have connections with important people."

Reva felt a surge of frustration. Nicola was using her husband's position at the bank to exert undue pressure, and it infuriated her. Nevertheless, she knew she had to tread carefully. She didn't need this to blow up and become worse.

"I understand your concerns, Nicola," Reva said, her voice measured. "Threats won't sway my decisions. I am here to serve the best interests of Thunder Mountain and its residents."

Nicola huffed in annoyance but seemed to back down slightly. "Fine, have it your way, Mayor. But don't expect the town meeting to be an easy one for you."

As Nicola turned to leave, Reva couldn't help feeling a mix of relief and apprehension. The upcoming town meeting was now set to be a battleground, and Reva knew she had to rally the support of her townspeople to stand firm against Nicola's attempts to manipulate the situation. That included Charlie Grace, Capri, and Lila.

While she knew she could count on her girlfriends to help, the responsibility to lead her town through the storm of emotions and conflict that lay ahead weighed squarely on her shoulders.

31

The midmorning sun cast a warm glow through the kitchen window as Charlie Grace sat down at the counter, sipping a cup of hot coffee and making a grocery list. She'd been up since the crack of dawn. She'd helped Aunt Mo with breakfast and clean-up. Then she'd helped Lizzy strip the beds in four of the cabins after guests had checked out. Horses had been fed. One of the saddles had a tear in the stirrup, so she'd need to take that to town for repair later today.

She placed the steaming mug down on the table, picked up a nearby pen, and went to work adding a list of things she'd need for a guided hike she planned on offering her guests. The Lupine Meadows Access Trail was living up to its name and was lined with mountain lupines in purple, yellow, white, and pink. While the trail was popular, it was also challenging—but worth the effort as it took trekkers up to Delta Lake with stunning panoramas of the valley below.

She'd written out several items on the paper tablet before her—bear spray, sunscreen, insect repellent, plenty of water—when her phone buzzed with a message from Reva.

"Emergency meeting at City Hall tonight. Urgent. Please meet me at the mayor's office as soon as possible," the message read. Charlie Grace noted the text was also sent to Capri and Lila.

Frowning with curiosity, Charlie Grace quickly replied, assuring Reva that she would be there. The meeting must be important for Reva to call them all together like this.

Charlie Grace stuffed the unfinished list in her jeans pocket, took a final sip from her mug, and headed for the sink where she dumped the remaining coffee down the drain. Then she grabbed her keys and headed for her car.

Arriving at the mayor's office, Charlie Grace was ushered into a small conference room where her friends gathered, heads bent in serious discussion.

"You go on in there, honey," Verna told her. "Something awful is brewing and the mayor needs your help."

It looked to be true as Charlie Grace glanced at the scene before her.

Reva appeared visibly tense, her brows furrowed with worry. Capri and Lila exchanged concerned glances.

"What's going on?" Charlie Grace asked, taking a seat beside Reva.

Reva took a deep breath. "You know about the television production Nick is working on, right? Well, there's been some unexpected opposition beyond what we'd anticipated. Apparently, Nicola Cavendish has rallied support for trying to shut down the production. She's convinced a number of people the production will disrupt the peace and harmony of Thunder Mountain."

"And she's telling everyone it will have a negative environmental impact," Lila added.

Charlie Grace scowled. "Can she do that? Shut it down?"

Capri nodded. "It's ridiculous! Nick's *Bear Country* production would bring more business to the town and put us on the map. My river rafting company is only one example of a business that would benefit."

"Some folks are worried about the changes it might bring," Lila explained. "They think it will attract the wrong crowd, bring in wealthy people who will buy vacation homes, and raise our housing costs, ultimately turning Thunder Mountain into another highly-populated tourist town with traffic jams and crowds. Like Jackson and Sun Valley."

"Or Aspen," Reva clarified. "That argument, if well made, would lead to tension among the locals...and invite in-fighting among our residents. Conflict that we don't need."

Charlie Grace listened attentively, her mind whirring with thoughts. She understood both sides of the argument. Thunder Mountain had always been a quiet, close-knit community, and any major change could be intimidating for some.

"They do know that the actual production is miles away—in Wilson?" she pointed out.

"That's still too close, according to Nicola. She claims our proximity and current lower real estate prices would migrate the influx to Thunder Mountain," Reva said, anxiety evident in her voice. "If this opposition gains momentum, it could split the town in two."

Lila nodded. "Just look at what is happening at the national level. I agree with Reva, if leadership doesn't stave this off, the residents of Thunder Mountain could end up angry and polarized. We don't want that."

Reva rubbed her forehead. "Exactly. Disagreements like this can be deeply personal, and potentially create wounds that take generations to heal."

Capri pulled her long blonde hair into a pony and knotted it at the back of her neck. "I talked to Pastor Pete when I heard rumbles of this over at the Rustic Pine. He mentioned change is inevitable. Yet, he believes it's essential to find a balance and address all these concerns head-on." She turned to Charlie

Grace. "Perhaps you could talk to Nick about the issues worrying folks...especially for those concerned about the film production's impact on the environment. I mean, I hear they've been granted a conditional use permit and will be filming inside the park?"

Charlie Grace leaned her arms over the table. "Pastor Pete has a point. Maybe some compromise could be reached to address the concerns and ensure the production benefits everyone. I'd like to help, but Nick left for Los Angeles yesterday."

"He's gone?" Reva asked.

"Afraid so."

"For how long?"

"He said he'd only be away for a couple of days." Charlie Grace glanced between her friends at the table. "I'd be happy to talk to him when he returns, but that doesn't do much to help with tonight's meeting." She grabbed her phone from her pocket. "I could text him if you think that would help."

Privately, she couldn't help but think about what this meant for her budding romance with Nick. If the film production was shut down, Nick might have to leave earlier than expected, and their time together would come to an abrupt halt.

Reva straightened. "Yeah, maybe you should give Nick a heads up. In the meantime, it's important we all show up for the meeting. Bring anyone who you think would support defusing Nicola's plans. She was wielding some hefty threats in my office. I wouldn't put it past her to try and have the permits pulled."

Charlie Grace's eyes widened. "Could she do that?"

Lila shook her head. "We all know she's connected to people in high places. Rumor has it she's been known to push Wooster into turning down loan requests to manipulate people around into her way of thinking."

Reva held up her open palms. "Okay, let's not borrow trouble. Let everyone show up and voice their opinions and hopefully, we'll find a way to reach a consensus."

"That's a good idea," Charlie Grace chimed in. "It'll give everyone a chance to be heard. Maybe Nicola will back down when she hears how many do not follow her lead."

The girls disbanded and promised to work hard to get a good attendance at the meeting. Even so, Charlie Grace's head buzzed with worry as she climbed into her pickup. Before she headed home, she texted Nick.

"Hey, I just came from a meeting with Reva. It appears there's some opposition to the television production prompting an emergency town hall meeting tonight. Call me when you can."

The future of Nick's production and, in some ways, Charlie Grace's blossoming romance hung in the balance. She couldn't help but feel that the decision reached that evening would shape not only the fate of the television production but also the course of her own heart.

32

The town hall stood dead center in the middle of Thunder Mountain, an aging wooden structure with a pitched roof and a clock tower, worn down by time and harsh Wyoming winters. Despite its age, the building was bursting at the seams with a crowd larger than any it had seen in years.

Coffee was brewing on a table in the back and the smell of freshly baked cookies permeated the air as the attendees made their way to metal folding chairs lined up facing a podium at the front of the room.

The room buzzed with chatter as Reva stood leaving Charlie Grace, Lila, and Capri seated, and made her way forward. She tapped a gavel on the podium, trying to hush the buzzing crowd.

"Let's get started, shall we?" she said into the scratchy-sounding microphone.

When she failed to gain the attention of everyone in the room, she pounded again—this time a little harder. "Could I please have your attention?"

That seemed to do the trick as all eyes drifted to the front of the room and a hush fell across the assembly.

"Thank you," Reva said. "And thank you all for coming out tonight." She cleared her throat. "As many of you may have heard, concerns have been raised about the television production near here. Let me say right up front that the city of Thunder Mountain has no official jurisdiction over the matter—"

Nicola Cavendish popped up from her chair, her voice surprisingly loud for someone of her petite stature. "Thunder Mountain may not have an official capacity in this situation, but we all know that official or not, we have the ability to influence what goes on in our area."

Capri leaned over to Charlie Grace and whispered, "Our area? The production is nearly fifty miles away."

Charlie Grace quietly nodded, then checked her phone for a response from Nick. She'd texted him several times since learning of the meeting with no reply. Puzzled, she pocketed her phone.

She turned her attention to the front where Reva tried to maintain an outward appearance of patience. Subtle cues in her expression and posture betrayed her growing irritation. "Thank you, Nicola. Let's keep an order to the meeting."

Not to be swayed, the banker's wife continued. "Thank you, Mayor. I'll go first. As most of you know, I insisted upon this emergency meeting because I believe our town's very existence is at stake. An influx of people will threaten our way of life and has the potential to turn our beloved Thunder Mountain into one more resort town. Housing prices and property taxes will skyrocket. Not to mention, the well-being of Grand Teton National Park is under threat. I learned many of the scenes will be filmed on the pristine shores of Jenny Lake." She gasped and her hand went to her chest. "Can you imagine the impact that will have?"

Brewster Findley pulled off his baseball cap and dusted it against one knee. "Did you say our property taxes will go up?"

From behind her, Charlie Grace heard Betty Dunning's frightened voice. "I can't afford that."

"Yeah, Thunder Mountain is our home, not a vacation rental," shouted Doc Strode. "None of us can shoulder extra taxes. Especially the residents of Thunder Mountain who are retired and on fixed incomes."

Reva squared her shoulders and held out open palms. "Please, let's not get ahead of things. While I agree that protections must be in place to address the issues raised, there are two sides to consider."

"Yeah," Brewster Findley shouted. "We can't neglect the fact that tourism will bring added income."

Capri stood. "I agree. It's inevitable that the production company will go forward with the filming of *Bear Country*. We're a little late in stopping it. The best we can hope for is to manage the impact and embrace the benefits," she reasoned.

"And not let this divide our town and cause turmoil," Charlie Grace added.

A few murmurs of agreement emanated from pockets of the crowd.

Nicola's eyes narrowed. "The television production, Bear Country, wants to use our lovely area as its set. Now, while some may see dollar signs, we need to think about the consequences," she argued.

Wooster Cavendish placed his hand on his wife's arm and attempted to pull her back into her seat...unsuccessfully.

Charlie Grace cleared her throat. "There's no evidence that the production company will harm the environment. I'm certain the permit issued included guardrails and strict standards. I'm also sure the production company promised to uphold all those standards."

"They always promise, Charlie Grace," Nicola countered,

her voice dripping with false sweetness. "But can we trust them?"

In a surprise move, Nicola pointed at Charlie Grace. "Besides, isn't your support for this project rather...personal? After all, you dumped poor Jason Griffith and nearly broke his heart so you could date the production designer on this project." She glanced around. "Where is Nick Thatcher, anyway? No doubt he's out at Teton Trails Guest Ranch with an open bottle of wine waiting for your return?"

Her harsh comment turned the room electric with tension. Both Lila and Capri stood. Before they could open their mouths to defend her, Charlie Grace parked her hands on her hips. "My support has nothing to do with my personal life."

Suddenly, a man's voice boomed from the back. "I have something to say."

All heads turned to see Clancy Rivers wheeling himself up to the front of the room. Aunt Mo remained at the back with her hand covering her mouth and her eyes wide.

Clancy stopped his wheelchair next to Nicola. He pointed his finger up at the shocked woman. "Enough, Nicola," he warned, his voice deep and gravelly. Despite being in a wheelchair, his presence filled the room. "If you have an issue with my daughter, you will have to take it up with me."

Charlie Grace's heart caught in her throat as her father spoke with a fervor she hadn't seen in years, especially since his accident. She could feel her pulse in her temples as her heart filled with a mixture of disbelief and a swell of shock at the deep-seated intensity of his reaction.

He swept an arm in the air. "Everyone here knows Charlotte Grace is one of the most hard-working, altruistic people in this room. In all of Thunder Mountain, for that matter. She has a brain in that head of hers, and if she voices support for something, you can bet her opinion is well thought out and considered." He gave his daughter's nemesis a grave look. "Never would she throw this town, or anyone in it, under the bus based on her feelings for a man."

The weight of their estrangement bore down on her making the air feel thick. Charlie Grace struggled to breathe as her father's response seeped deep inside her.

She had prepared herself for the town's reactions—and even for Nicola's barbs—though she was startled when they were directed at her. Nothing could have readied her for this unexpected show of support from the one man she thought she had lost, evidenced by so much disdain and anger for her choices regarding the ranch. Each word he spoke in her defense chipped away at the wall she'd built around her emotions and left her reeling.

He turned, and their eyes met. Fighting tears, she mouthed, "Thank you."

Clancy turned back to Nicola, who looked taken aback as she murmured, "I merely meant that—"

"That what?" Clancy challenged, with a glint of mischief in his eye. "That you're worried about the lake's purity? Isn't that the same lake you used to skinny-dip in during your wilder days? I know where the birthmark is. Or have you forgotten that?"

A ripple of laughter spread through the town hall. Many of the attendees had been around long enough to remember the stories of young Nicola's escapades. Even Reva suppressed a chuckle.

Nicola's face turned beet red, her lips quivering with a mixture of anger and embarrassment. "That was years ago! This is about the environment!"

Clancy raised an eyebrow. "Seems to me, the lake survived you. I reckon it'll survive a television crew."

Reva banged her gavel, attempting to restore order to the now-laughing audience. "All right, enough. Let's remember we're here to discuss the agenda."

As the crowd started to settle, it was clear that Clancy had managed to defuse some of the tension in the room and in doing so, had shifted the scales in favor of the production.

Fleet Southcott glanced around. "Seems to me we should give the production company a chance. No one's proven they are hurting the environment. As far as the growth issue, we can cocoon ourselves and try to stave off growth but reality dictates that isn't entirely possible. Fact is, none of us is forced to sell to outsiders. That's an individual choice."

Dot Montgomery nodded in agreement. "I concur. If we had chosen to stop tourism ten years back, then many of our current businesses wouldn't have been able to open their doors."

Donna Hatfield leaned forward in her chair and addressed the crowd. "We can simply manage the influx of business and let our town be known for its welcome mat."

The townspeople started to gather their things. Some stood.

Looking relieved, Reva surveyed the room. "Anyone else wish to express themselves on this matter?"

Most shook their heads no and some started heading for the door.

Reva leaned toward the microphone. "Do I have a motion to table this matter?"

Both Capri and Lila quickly responded in unison. "I make the motion." They looked at each other and laughed.

Verna Billingsley sat at a nearby table with her pencil poised above a lined tablet, trying to record the minutes. She had a big smile on her face.

"Fine," Reva announced. "Unless I hear an objection, we'll table this matter. Is that agreeable with you, Nicola?"

When her detractor crossed her arms and remained silent, Reva pounded the gavel. "This meeting is adjourned."

Nicola stood, huffed, and marched from the town hall. Her husband, Wooster, followed close behind, chuckling.

Charlie Grace made her way to her father's side, her eyes brimming with tears. She leaned down, placing a gentle hand on Clancy's shoulder. "I appreciate what you did, Dad," she whispered.

Clancy just nodded. He grabbed his daughter's hand and gave it a squeeze.

The townsfolk dispersed, some heading towards the refreshment table, others sharing chuckles over Nicola's skinny-dipping revelation. Fleet Southcott waited for Wooster and Nicola to depart, and then he approached Clancy as Aunt Mo wheeled him toward the door. He had a mischievous twinkle in his eye. "Hey, Clancy. I've got a new dessert idea for the menu down at the Rustic Pine. How about 'Nicola's Skinny-Dip Sundae'?"

He noticed Pete Cumberland a few yards away. "Sorry, Pastor."

The room filled with another round of laughter. Charlie Grace shook her head as she stood by her father's wheelchair, trying to stifle her giggles as they headed for the door.

As the echoes of mirth faded into the cool night, she was reminded once again that Thunder Mountain was more than just a place on the map. It was a town where every corner felt like home and every face was family.

33

Jewel grabbed a freshly baked cinnamon roll from the plate on the kitchen table. "I love Saturdays, Mom!"

Charlie Grace grinned. "You do? Why?"

Her daughter nodded. "Because I get to stay home from school and play cards with Grandpa!"

Clancy appeared in the doorway. He wheeled himself to the table. "Did I hear my name?"

"Grandpa! I have the cards all shuffled and ready to go." She turned to Charlie Grace. "Mom, Grandpa taught me to shuffle. Want me to show you?"

Charlie Grace grinned at her father. "Sure, baby. I'm watching." With a stack of unopened mail in her hand, she headed for the table and took a seat across from her father. "Hungry, Dad?"

He reached for a cinnamon roll. "Yeah. These look good. I love Mo's rolls."

"I made them, Dad. Using her recipe, of course." She waited for the barb that normally came.

"Well, good for you!"

Stunned, she smiled and started opening an envelope.

"Momma, watch!" Jewel took the cards and split them into two stacks. Her brow furrowed in concentration as she lifted the stacks carefully in her two small hands.

"Slow," Clancy warned. "Don't get in a hurry."

Jewel nodded. She held the stacks and riffled them together, allowing the cards to interweave. "There! I did it!"

Charlie Grace beamed. "You sure did."

Jewel leaped from her seat and threw her arms around her grandpa. "Thanks for teaching me."

A smile nipped at the corners of Clancy's lips. "Let's see if you remember what I taught you about Rummy."

"Oh, I remember," Jewel said, taking her seat. She lifted the deck of cards and began dealing them. "And I'm going to kick your fanny."

"Hey, language," Charlie Grace warned.

Jewel shrugged with remorse. "Sorry, Mom."

Charlie Grace focused her attention on the contents of the envelope. It was a bill for feed—a large one. She tucked it aside. While the guest ranch was in the black, there wasn't a lot of room for error. The bill was more than she expected, and she'd have to do some juggling to pay it.

The next envelope on the stack of unopened mail was small and made of what looked to be expensive paper—some kind of thick linen and it was sealed with a gold sticker in the shape of a pineapple.

Curious, she slid her fingers under the glued flap and opened it, then withdrew a beautiful card made of the same paper, embossed with a border of tiny gold pineapples and scented. She brought the card to her nose. It smelled like a pina colada.

"What's that?" her dad asked.

"Looks like a thank-you card." Her eyes scanned the beautiful handwriting.

"Thank you so very much for the lovely time we had at Teton

Trails. Everything was perfect—from the glorious mountain setting, the wildlife, the sweet cabin and accouterments, and especially the food. We had a marvelous stay! (We'll be telling everyone we know and urging them to visit. We also plan on returning in the future.) All our love, Ava and Tom Strobbe"

Charlie Grace couldn't help herself. Her face broke into a wide grin.

Her dad picked up his cards and arranged them in his hand. "So? Who's it from?"

"Ava and Tom Strobbe. They visited us all the way from Maui."

"Maui?"

"Yeah, they wanted to extend their gratitude for a lovely stay." The smile wouldn't leave her face.

"Well, ain't that something?" Her dad placed a matched set of cards down on the table in front of him and drew from the pile.

"Yeah, good for you, Grandpa," Charlie Grace repeated, wondering if he caught the double meaning of her accolade. She wasn't sure what had prompted this sudden change in his attitude toward her and the guest ranch, but she was grateful.

Her gaze drifted to the wall clock. "Oh, my gosh. Is it really getting that late?" She pushed the rest of the unopened mail aside, intending to deal with it later. Then she stood and stuffed the feed bill in her back pocket. Before paying that amount, she'd like to check with Gibbs and see if there was an explanation for the rise in cost. Had he purchased some other type of feed without her approval?

She kissed the top of Jewel's head. "You have fun with Grandpa. I have some stuff I've got to take care of." She moved for the sink, grabbed a glass from the cupboard, and filled it. Gazing outside, she noticed Gibbs' truck. Good, at least he wasn't late again.

She downed the water and placed the empty glass in the

dishwasher. "I'll see you later," she said as she headed out the door.

As she entered the barn, a quiet murmur of voices caught her attention.

Charlie Grace glanced around. No sign of Gibbs.

Gentle laughter coming from the hay loft told her all she needed to know. She took a deep breath, summoning her ability to remain calm, and made her way to the ladder leading up to the loft.

She climbed onto the ladder, taking one rung at a time, growing angrier by the second as it became clear one of the voices was a woman.

That man had some nerve!

Gibbs had crossed a lot of lines, but he wasn't about to participate in hanky-panky on her time...and paycheck!

She reached the top and carefully peered over to where the sounds were coming from. Stunned at what she saw, she lifted herself up and parked her hands on her hips.

There, amidst the hay bales, were Gibbs and Lizzy Cayman, their faces flushed, caught in an intimate moment. A pang of outrage tore through Charlie Grace.

She could have shouted or caused a scene, but instead she chose quiet strength. Taking a moment to compose herself, she cleared her throat.

Gibbs' eyes widened and Lizzy, her face red as a ripe apple, scrambled to cover herself. "Charlie Grace," Gibbs stammered, clearly caught off guard.

"Of all the places, Gibbs," Charlie Grace said, her voice steady. "And people." She looked at Lizzy.

Lizzy, flustered, tried to speak. "Charlie Grace, I—"

"Charlie Grace, this isn't what it looks like," Gibbs attempted to explain, his voice desperate.

She raised an eyebrow, a small smile tugging at the corner

of her mouth. "Really? Because from where I stand, it looks like two people making very poor choices."

Lizzy at least had the decency to look down in shame. "Please don't tell Uncle Albie. I mean, if he knew—"

Charlie Grace shook her head. "Albie and I go way back. He's a good man."

Gibbs tried again. "Charlie Grace, I'm sorry. Please don't tell Albie."

She held up a hand, silencing him. "Save it, Gibbs. Save your apologies and excuses. I've heard them all before. And honestly, it's not about me anymore. I couldn't care less who you spend time with—clothes or not. But not on my time."

There was a pregnant pause, the weight of regret and reflection hanging in the air.

Charlie Grace turned to Lizzy as the girl scrambled back into her clothes. "Lizzy, you're young. I hope you find what you're looking for in life, but it isn't in a barn with your boss's ex-husband."

The girl was stupid enough to simply shrug.

"By the way...you are both fired. I'll get your final paychecks ready."

Lizzy parked her hands on her hips. "Fired? You can't do that."

"I think I just did." And, with that, Charlie Grace left the barn and returned to the house, her resolve even stronger.

She was in the kitchen only a minute when the back door flew open, and Gibbs raced inside. "Charlie Grace, we need to talk."

"We're done talking." Charlie Grace patted Jewel on the shoulder. "Honey, go outside and play, please."

"But, Mom. I'm about to win," her daughter argued.

"The cards can stay on the table. Go outside. You can resume your game with Grandpa in a little while."

Her daughter glanced between her parents and seemed to

recognize the gravity of the moment. She sighed. "Well, don't fight."

"Go," Charlie Grace said and pointed to the door.

As soon as Jewel was safely out of earshot, Gibbs launched into trying to change Charlie Grace's mind. "Look, I know it looks bad. But we're both adults. You're overreacting."

"You're both employees using my time for personal...uh, matters."

She glanced over at her dad, waiting for him to come to Gibbs' rescue. Strangely, he held his tongue.

She marched into the office with Gibbs trailing her. "Look, okay...maybe that wasn't the best decision, but you can't fire us."

"I can, and I did," she told him, repeating what she'd said to Lizzy earlier. She retrieved the business checkbook from the desk drawer. She plopped it down, grabbed a pen, and quickly made out two checks, calculating the amount due in her head. She tore the checks out of the book and turned to face him.

That's when she noticed her dad in his wheelchair only feet away.

So did Gibbs. He turned to her father. "Clancy, talk some sense into her, will you? Who's going to feed and make beds if she cans the people employed to help her?"

Her father wheeled slightly closer. "Were you messing with the help on company time?"

Gibbs rubbed the back of his neck. "Well, yeah...but—"

Charlie Grace winced at his lack of ability to accept responsibility for what he'd done. "Lizzy Cayman is years younger than you. And my employee. And Albie Barton's niece." She shook her head in disgust. "Some things never change."

Ignoring her, Gibbs continued to make his case to Clancy. "This is a minor infraction. Nothing that deserves termination." He pointed back at Charlie Grace. "She's working off emotion here, just like always."

Clancy's face darkened.

Gibbs frowned. "Clancy, tell her." There was desperation in his eyes.

"Son," Clancy began, with a steady tone that demanded attention. "I listened to my daughter cry night after night because of what you did to her. I heard her heartbreak. Now, it's not my place to tell her how to feel or what to decide. She gave you another chance...in fact, more than one. Foolishly, I'm to blame for some of that." He harrumphed. "Trust is like fine china—once broken, you can glue the pieces, but it's never the same again, no matter how well you try to mend it. Sadly, it appears you think you can keep slamming the china piece down believing she's obligated to reglue it again and again."

Clancy looked at Charlie Grace, then back at Gibbs. "Whatever she decides, you're going to have to respect it."

Charlie Grace blinked, taken aback by her father's words. Always the traditionalist, he had previously been quick to insist that she should forgive, attributing Gibbs' transgression to "men being men" and emphasizing the sanctity of marriage above all else. Countless times she'd met with resistance and outdated ideologies. After his accident, his attitude became worse. He grew extremely critical of everything she did, every decision.

Now, seeing him stand firmly by her side valuing her decision, she felt a warmth spread within her. That, coupled with his support at the town hall meeting, caused tears to well—not of sorrow, but of gratitude for his newfound respect.

Once again, they shared a gaze. He smiled at her and the walls between father and daughter, built by years of discord, seemed to crumble in that singular, profound moment. She didn't understand his sudden attitude change, but she relished his respect and support.

Gibbs took the check from her hand. He glanced between her and her father, stunned at the new development.

Gibbs was Jewel's father—that would never change. Charlie Grace had committed long ago to do whatever it took to preserve that relationship for her daughter. That didn't mean she had to let Gibbs step all over her.

"Well, I guess I should go." Gibbs, still looking confused, turned for the door.

"Gibbs?" she said.

He turned to face her, his expression immediately hopeful. "Yeah?"

"Here, take Lizzy's check out to her."

"Oh, yeah. Okay." He plucked the check from her hand. Their eyes met briefly. Charlie Grace forced herself not to look away.

Finally, he turned for the door a second time.

Charlie Grace rested her hand on her father's shoulder and watched through the open door as Gibbs lifted Jewel into his arms and gave her a kiss. There was a brief verbal exchange, and then he put her back on the ground and walked toward Lizzy, who now stood by his truck, waiting.

34

C harlie Grace's fingers hovered over the glass panes of the Jackson Hole Airport as she watched the private jet land gracefully, then taxi in from the runway. Within minutes the jet came to a stop and orange-vested airport attendants wheeled a ramp to the plane's door. The door opened and passengers began appearing on the tiny metal landing, including Nick's unmistakable silhouette.

Dressed in a white button-down shirt, sleeves pushed up, and a leather jacket draped nonchalantly over one shoulder, Nick exuded a raw confidence that still managed to catch her off-guard.

As he crossed the tarmac on his way to the gate, their eyes met across the distance, a magnetic pull drawing her towards the arrival gate. His lips lifted in a small smile, and he raised a hand in a subtle wave as he watched her through the window.

She waved back and quickly crossed the shiny concrete floor flanked by walls made of timber and weathered steel. She stood at the gate with impatience, waiting for him to appear.

"Hey," he murmured as they met, drawing her into an

embrace that spoke of longing. "I missed you." The depth in his eyes told her he meant every word.

She leaned into him, breathing in his familiar earthy scent. "I missed you, too. How was the trip?"

"Productive. But I'm glad to be back." He took her hand in his. "We had turbulence on the flight, which limited cabin service. I haven't eaten. Are you hungry?" He pointed to the food kiosks.

"Starving, but let's head to Jedediah's. It's a grab-n-go restaurant but has seating. I can grab some sourdough starter to take home. Don't tell Aunt Mo, but I ruined her starter by forgetting to feed it."

He laughed. "Won't she know?"

"Oh, yes," she assured. "But she won't say anything."

The gentle hum of the airport, the muted conversations, all faded away as she focused on Nick by her side as they made their way to the restaurant which was located at the far end of the small terminal and was surprisingly packed for this time of day. They headed for an empty table in the back, next to the counter.

Charlie Grace listened intently as Nick recounted his trip, sharing the highlights of being back in Los Angeles and the downsides. "I'd forgotten how snarled the traffic gets on the freeways," he told her. "I came to appreciate small-town living a little more with the sound of every blasting horn."

"Well, there are downsides to small towns as well." She reminded him about the town hall meeting.

"Look, I'm so sorry I didn't respond to your texts promptly. I was completely wrapped up with a business associate. When I did finally break free, my phone battery was running low, and I forgot to pack my charger." He grinned. "Yes, I'm one of those guys who never carries an extra. I would have called, but it was late, and I didn't want to wake you."

"No problem," she told him. "You got back to me when you

could. Sorry about the charger. Admittedly, I've done the same."

"I had to climb in the car and go buy one. Anyway, by the next morning, you'd already messaged telling me the pushback on the production was resolved." He laughed. "Looks like there was drama while I was gone."

She grinned and plucked a menu from its holder on the table. "High drama. But, like I told you, everything ended well."

"I have to admit something," he draped his jacket across the back of the chair. "I wasn't even sure I should tell you," he began, drawing in a deep breath, his gaze serious.

"Oh?" Her curiosity was raised. "What's that?"

"I called Nicola Cavendish after you and I texted the next morning. I invited her to come out to the set...as an extra. She couldn't accept fast enough. Seems she no longer has any trouble with *Bear Country* filming in the area."

Charlie Grace opened her mouth in shock. "You devil!"

"No, just a production designer trying to smooth things over. Seems the lady was pretty taken with the chance to be on film."

Charlie Grace was completely tickled by the revelation and couldn't wait to tell Reva and the others. And her dad.

Nick looked across the table at her, amused by her expression of shock. "Doesn't hurt to use any tool necessary. Now, what else did I miss?"

She took the opportunity to tell Nick about her dad at the meeting and his unexpected support. "He wasn't the man I've lived with since the accident. He was...well, he was like my old dad."

Nick beamed. "I'm so glad to hear that." He reached across the table and cupped her hand in his. "I know that must mean so much to you."

"There's more," she said. She told him about having to fire Gibbs and Lizzy...and why.

"Ouch."

"How'd her uncle take it?"

"He was terribly disappointed. And embarrassed. He kept apologizing for Lizzy's actions."

"He wasn't responsible," Nick noted.

"No, of course not. But Albie seems to have a blind spot when it comes to his sister's daughter. He's very fond of her. I only wish she appreciated her uncle's affection and the way he looks after her best interests." She took a deep breath. "The bright side is that my dad supported my decision. Lock, stock, and barrel."

"I bet that felt good, given everything you've told me."

She nodded. "It does feel good, Nick. A huge weight has lifted. We even talk at breakfast, and he's no longer critical. I mean, miracles do happen, I guess."

A pleased grin lifted the corners of Nick's lips. "You warrant every good thing that comes your way, Charlie Grace. You deserve to be happy."

She smiled and handed him a menu. Overhead, a departing flight number was called over the intercom as she delivered their orders to the counter.

Nick had a meatball sub, and Charlie Grace ordered a huckleberry chicken sandwich. They talked little as they both scarfed down the delicious fare. Minutes later, Nick pushed his empty plate aside. "Boy, that hit the spot! I was really hungry."

The truth was, Charlie Grace was as well. Not for the food. She'd been hungry to see Nick again, and she told him so.

"I feel the same," he admitted as he reached for her hand again.

Something in the way he looked at her made her heart idle a little too fast.

An older couple made their way to the neighboring table. The man pulled out the chair with veined hands and waited for his spouse to be seated before kissing the top of her white hair.

"My trip had a purpose." He squeezed her hand. "I have some news."

She found it hard to breathe, suddenly filled with worry. "News?" She reached for her glass with her free hand and took a drink, hoping to wet the sudden parched feeling building in her throat.

Was he leaving Wyoming earlier than thought?

He squeezed her hand. "When I was in L.A., I met with a woman I know—Barbara Corcoran."

She nearly spit out the drink. "*The* Barbara Corcoran? Like that lady on television." She snapped her fingers. "What was the name of that show?"

"*Shark Tank.*"

Charlie Grace slapped the table, her nerves getting the better of her. "Yes, *Shark Tank*. Oh, my goodness, you know her?"

As soon as the words were out of her mouth, she wanted to gobble them back. He was in the film industry. Of course, he hobknobbed with celebrities.

"I needed some advice."

This time Charlie Grace had the good sense to exercise restraint. She nodded and acted as though it was no big deal to be friends with a multi-millionaire who was known across America. Even more, she stomped down her hidden worry that his news might not be what she wanted to hear.

He grinned. "Don't get impressed."

She quickly bobbed her head in agreement. "No, exactly. No big deal."

Nick's smile broadened. "As you know, Barbara is known for her business acumen, especially in real estate."

"Oh?"

He continued to grin. "We're neighbors," he confided.

She let out a deep breath. "Not just friends. Neighbors," she repeated.

Nick seemed to draw immense pleasure from her being starstruck.

"I suppose you spend the holidays with Ben Affleck and Jennifer Lopez."

His silence hit her between the eyes. "Wait...you know them? You're acquainted with the famous *Bennifer*?"

He shrugged. "It's no big deal. But no, I won't be spending the holidays in L.A. I hope to enjoy the snow this year. Do the whole winter scene thing for Christmas...you know, the horse-drawn sleigh, skiing the slopes, and roasting chestnuts on an open fire."

He paused, gazed at her intently. "I wanted Barbara's advice on selling my house in Pacific Palisades."

Charlie Grace eyed Nick. "What are you saying?"

Nick's gaze bore into hers, filled with a vulnerability she had only seen a few times before. "I've been doing a lot of thinking. Reflecting, if you will. Every moment away from here, from you, only solidified where my heart truly belongs. I want to make a life here...permanently. I listed my place."

She stilled. "You're selling your house?

He smiled from across the table. "I want to make Wyoming my permanent home."

Emotion welled up as she processed his words. The man who had reignited her passion and hope in life wanted to be with her. The weight of the realization settled deep within her, filling spaces she didn't even know were empty.

"Nick, this is...it's a big step. Are you sure?"

Nick looked deep into her eyes, the weight of his own emotion evident. "You know, I never saw it coming, Charlie Grace. The idea of finding love seemed like something out of the movies, an elusive thing that never happens in real life. But then you walked into my life, and everything shifted. I've treasured every shared laugh, every whispered secret, it's brought a clarity I never knew I was missing."

The news was thrilling, but as she processed his words, she couldn't help but turn to the practical implications. "What about your job?"

"I can work from anywhere. Thunder Mountain will be my home base. I'll continue to travel for extended periods, as necessary. I'd change even that if I could, but my trips are not up for negotiation. At least not until I can retire, which I plan to do as early as possible."

Reaching across the table, she touched his face, fingers tracing the familiar lines. "Nick, are you sure?"

He stood and came around to her, lifted her from her chair, and pulled her into an embrace. "Absolutely, I plan to spend every possible minute with you."

Charlie Grace flung herself at Nick, arms twining up around his neck, fingers tangled in the deep brown shock of his hair. She kissed him hungrily, her mouth, her body, every ounce of her being caught up in the moment.

The older couple sitting at the nearby table smiled at them.

She had never seen this coming. Even so, she was delighted she wouldn't have to bid Nick and their romance goodbye.

While hard for her to admit, the notion of happiness had eluded her for much of her adult life. Oh sure, she'd enjoyed many good things in life. But she'd also spent years wrestling with uncertainty, frequently second-guessing her choices, and feeling perpetually let down by life. The struggle to find personal happiness had been a constant uphill battle.

Now, having finally found deep joy, the sensation was unexpectedly grounding. It was less about elation and more about a sense of balance and contentment. She'd learned that she could see to the needs of others without putting herself on the back burner...especially when it came to relationships.

Nick Thatcher had a lot to do with that. He'd given her the gift of believing in herself.

Better yet, he'd given her the gift of love.

35

The boat bobbed gently on Jenny Lake's tranquil waters, the peaks of the Tetons mirrored perfectly on the surface. Lila, her fingers trailing in the cool water, turned to Charlie Grace with a wistful smile, "Do you remember when we camped here back in high school? And Capri forgot to pack the tent poles?"

Capri chuckled. "Hey! We made do with those pine limbs and a bit of creativity. Created an unforgettable trip, didn't it?"

Reva leaned back, shading her eyes from the soft glint of the sun. "Every time we're here, it feels like the mountains hold our memories. Sometimes, I swear I can hear our younger selves laughing in the wind." She reached for the champagne bottle. "Who's up for some celebration?"

Lila unpacked the plastic flutes and passed them out. "What are we celebrating?"

Charlie Grace nodded with enthusiasm. "We're celebrating us. We've all experienced changes over the years, been blindsided by unexpected circumstances, and we've held on to the possibility of renewed hope...and each other."

Reva popped the cork. "Some of us more than others." She directed her gaze at Charlie Grace.

"Who are you looking at?" Charlie Grace challenged.

"You," came Reva's reply. She poured bubbly into all their waiting glasses. "This has certainly been a summer of change for you."

Charlie Grace took a moment, gathering her thoughts. "I guess you're right. I think back to how I used to be, especially with Gibbs. I let him and his bad choices dictate so much of my life." She stared at the bubbles drifting to the top of her glass. "Through it all, our friendship—and my new friendship with Nick—gave me the strength to stand up for myself and find happiness."

She sighed, a hint of a smile forming. "I never imagined I could find someone like him after everything. He's been a genuine, unexpected joy in my life. Falling in love with him feels right, and it's made all the difference."

Reva lifted her glass and filled it. "What's hard to wrap my head around is the change in your father."

Charlie Grace sighed. "Yes, I'll live a lifetime wondering what brought about his change of heart."

Capri shrugged. "I know."

Everyone turned their focus on her.

"What do you mean, you know?" Lila asked.

Capri leaned back and kicked her feet up on the edge of the boat. "I know why Clancy softened and quit being a poop to Charlie Grace."

Charlie Grace leaned forward. "Well, you'd better spill."

Capri let her gaze drift to the horizon, the sun casting a canvas of pinks and golds across the tips of the pines. "Dick paid him a visit."

Lila's eyebrows lifted. "Your stepdad?"

"Yeah, Dick didn't tell me what was said verbatim, but let's just say he conveyed the notion that time is short and none of us is promised tomorrow. He told me and Mom he urged Clancy to quit being a jackass and making his daughter miserable. That one day, he'd be gone and never missed. Worse, his daughter might be the one not there, and he'd never get the opportunity to say he was sorry and tell her he loved her."

"Oh, my gosh...what did Clancy say?" Reva asked.

"Charlie Grace's dad is a man of few words...or no words. I suppose his actions speak louder. No doubt, it looks like Dick's admonition prompted an about-face."

Charlie Grace let the new information settle. It made sense now. Regardless of the motivation, she was sincerely glad for her father's change of heart towards her. Slowly, they were becoming close again. It meant the world to her.

"Well, ain't that something?" Reva raised her plastic flute and invited the others to do the same. "I want to make a toast. To the moments that break us, and the friends who make us."

The others raised their glasses in response, and for a brief moment, everything else faded away. All that remained was the heartbeat of their friendship, pulsing stronger than ever, a promise that whatever came next, they would face it together.

Capri suddenly stood, sending the boat rocking. She tossed back the champagne in her glass and quickly disrobed.

"What are you doing?" Lila demanded.

"I'm going skinny-dipping!"

"Now?" Lila asked.

"Yes, now. Is there a better time?" Capri dove into the water, turned, and waved for them to follow. "C'mon, what are you waiting for?"

"We're grown women," Lila argued.

"But we're not old." Capri dove deep, letting her feet escape the surface of the water.

The three women left in the boat glanced around.

Seeing no one within viewing distance, Reva shrugged. "What the heck?" She stripped down and dove in. Laughing from the water, she gleefully yelled out, "Here's to Nicola Cavendish!"

Capri's head bobbed up through the surface of the water in time to add, "And to tattoos!"

Next was Lila, first taking care to fold her clothes. "I can't believe we're doing this." Naked, she held her nose and jumped into the water.

That left Charlie Grace in the boat. She grinned and unsnapped her jeans, pulled them off, and took off her shirt. "What the heck!"

Life was good. Especially when she had the love of good friends, family, and now Nick.

She was diving in!

READY FOR MORE OF the Teton Mountain Series? Check out book two: ECHOES OF THE HEART and read about Reva's surprise adventure.

AUTHOR'S NOTE

Hello, Readers!

A heartfelt thank you for reading the Teton Mountain Series. These books celebrate the invaluable role of friendships. I am thankful to have girlfriends I've known since high school. These women bless me beyond what I can describe.

The spark for these stories was my own experiences of profound friendship, a theme I've always wanted to explore in my writing.

A trip to Yellowstone National Park and the Teton Mountain National Park in Wyoming inspired the setting. For any of you who have followed me, you know I thrill to take my readers to places I love to vacation. In these books, you'll be whisked away to the majestic Teton Mountains, you'll dine in the trendy restaurants in Jackson Hole, and see bears and moose in secluded pinewood forests. You'll experience herds of buffalo roaming the meadows of Hayden Valley and hike the back-country trails around crystal blue lakes lined with pastel-colored lupine blooms. The town of Thunder Mountain is a fictionalized community based upon DuBois, Wyoming—a charming western town with wooden boardwalks and quaint buildings lining its Main Street. I took a some liberty as an author and relocated it to where Moran is now on the map.

Mostly, I created four women friends who have found a place in my own heart as I've placed them on the pages of these books—Charlie Grace, Reva, Lila and Capri.

I hope you enjoy the time spent with us!

Kellie Coates Gilbert

ALSO BY KELLIE COATES GILBERT

TETON MOUNTAIN SERIES
Where We Belong – Book 1
Echoes of the Heart – Book 2
Holding the Dream – Book 3
As the Sun Rises – Book 4

MAUI ISLAND SERIES
Under the Maui Sky – Book 1
Silver Island Moon – Book 2
Tides of Paradise – Book 3
The Last Aloha – Book 4
Ohana Sunrise – Book 5
Sweet Plumeria Dawn – Book 6
Songs of the Rainbow – Book 7
Hibiscus Christmas – Book 8

PACIFIC BAY SERIES
Chances Are – Book 1
Remember Us – Book 2
Chasing Wind – Book 3

Between Rains – Book 4

SUN VALLEY SERIES
Sisters – Book 1
Heartbeats – Book 2
Changes – Book 3
Promises – Book 4

TEXAS GOLD COLLECTION
A Woman of Fortune – Book 1
Where Rivers Part – Book 2
A Reason to Stay – Book 3
What Matters Most – Book 4

STAND ALONE NOVELS:

Mother of Pearl

AVAILABLE AT ALL MAJOR RETAILERS

FOR EXCLUSIVE DISCOUNTS:

www.kelliecoatesgilbertbooks.com

SNEEK PEEK ~ ECHOES OF THE HEART

Chapter 1

"Pull!"

As the clay pigeon launched into the air, Reva Nygard tracked the bright orange disk with laser focus. Her finger tightened on the trigger, and with a resounding bang, she shattered the target. The crowd erupted in applause.

Capri Jacobs, one of her best friends from high school, stood nearby, a grin on her face. "Way to show 'em what you're made of."

Reva's face displayed every bit of her delight. "Thanks, Capri," she replied, reloading her shotgun with ease.

The scent of freshly fired gunpowder hung in the air as Reva stepped back up to the shooting station at the Thunder Mountain gun range, her boots sinking slightly into the soft ground as she found her stance. Her long black hair dangled in a braid down her back as she nodded, the cool confidence she often exuded in the courtroom now directed toward the blue horizon.

A second clay pigeon shot into the air. Reva tracked it with unerring focus, her trigger finger curling around metal. Time seemed to slow as she followed the orange disc's trajectory, and then, with fluid grace, she shot.

A deafening bang resonated through the valley as the shotgun unleashed its payload. Reva's target disintegrated into a cloud of orange dust, the remnants scattering like stardust against the vibrant backdrop of the Teton Mountains.

The townspeople gathered at the event cheered. A fellow shooter and the town veterinarian, Tillman Strode, shook his head. "Great shot, Reva," he said, admiration in his voice.

Reva's heart swelled with pride, her keen senses soaking in the scent of pine needles and damp earth mixed with the heady aroma of chili cooking. In the distance, Oma Griffith, Betty Dunning, and Dorothy Vaughn—known as the Knit Wits to everyone in Thunder Mountain—waved their spoons and ladles in a show of solidarity before returning to dishing up bowls and handing them out.

Competition was stiff here at the annual skeet shoot and chili cook-off. Not only were the best local marksmen lined up to compete, but some serious cooks were standing over simmering pots guarding their secret ingredients. The funds raised would go to charity. This year's money would help remodel the community center, a place where both seniors and youth could gather.

"I think you've got this," Capri leaned and lowered her voice, cupping her mouth with her hand. "Doc Tillman is your only real rival, and he seems to be losing his focus. You've got him doubting himself."

"You think so?" Reva whispered back. She rarely let her proclivity for conquering her opponents take backstage—even when there seemed to be so little at stake.

Reva's affinity for victory was undeniable. Winning was simply in her DNA, a reflection of her unwavering determination and unrelenting pursuit of excellence.

She'd once been accused of not knowing how to relax. Perhaps true, but she loved giving life one hundred percent every waking hour. Especially now when her efforts served the residents of her beloved Thunder Mountain. As mayor, she could think of no better focus than on her neighbors and friends.

The final round came down to the wire, with Reva managing to maintain her lead.

As that last clay pigeon disintegrated in the air, she knew she had done it. She could easily win this competition, impressing the crowd, and herself as well. She'd already pulled off a personal best, shooting forty-seven out of fifty—a feat anyone would be proud of. Now, only one more to go to complete victory.

The sun began to dip in the sky and the mountains perched as silhouettes against the fading sunlight. A hushed anticipation settled over the attendees as the organizers gathered at the makeshift podium, where a gleaming trophy awaited its rightful owner.

Reva, her heart pounding with exhilaration, stood alongside the other competitors, including Doc Tillman. Capri waved from the crowd, beaming with pride. The scent of victory was palpable. She rarely missed a shot in all her years of competing.

Reva squinted under the bright sky, her finger resting lightly on the trigger. Out of the corner of her eye, she caught sight of Doc Tillman's hopeful eyes. The clay pigeon launched, a fleeting target against the vast blue.

With a gentle sigh, she subtly adjusted her aim. The shot rang out, echoing her decision across the field. The orange disk sailed away unscathed, and a surprised cheer erupted for the beloved veterinarian.

Albie Barton, the newspaper editor, served as the tournament announcer. He cleared his throat and raised the award high. "Ladies and gentlemen, we have a winner," he declared, his voice carrying across the range. "With an incredible display of marksmanship, our very own Doc Tillman has claimed the title of the Thunder Mountain skeet shooting champion!"

Everyone burst into cheers and applause, clapping their hands and whistling in appreciation. Reva's cheeks flushed with the warmth of their admiration for a man who deserved every bit of the honor. She couldn't help but smile as he accepted the shiny trophy, shaped like a stylized clay pigeon in mid-flight.

Doc Tillman held the prize close, his eyes glistening with a mix of gratitude and accomplishment. "Thank you, everyone," he exclaimed. "This means the world to me."

"Congratulations, Reva!" Capri whispered as she threw her arms around her friend in a tight hug. "You did it!"

Reva scowled. "What are you talking about?"

Capri grinned. "You have a sneaky habit of stepping aside to let others pass you."

She shrugged and smiled back. "People who take the high road encounter less traffic."

Capri squeezed Reva's shoulders. "Let's get us a bowl of chili, then we'll head out to Teton Trails and celebrate the news of your non-win with Lila and Charlie Grace." Capri held up her phone. "I've been texting with them. Lila is at the ranch helping Charlie Grace birth that calf that's giving her trouble."

The two women linked arms and approached the tables lined with simmering pots of chili, the spicy aromas mingling in the air. "Well, what have we here?" Reva said, stopping in front of the Knit Wit ladies.

Oma Griffith immediately scooped a sample of their entry into a disposable paper bowl and handed it to Reva with a spoon. "We know you like chocolate and—"

Betty Dunning gave her a sharp elbow jab. "Shh...that's our secret ingredient."

Dorothy Vaughn rolled her eyes. "Well, not now, it isn't."

Oma's expression immediately filled with horror. "I—I didn't mean to—"

Reva leaned close. "No worries. Your secret is safe with the mayor."

Capri failed to suppress a chuckle despite covering her mouth with her hand. "Uh, with me too. I won't tell."

The promise seemed to bring some relief to the ladies across the table.

"So, what do you think?" Dorothy urged.

Reva tasted the chili and gave an appreciative groan. "Oh, it's delicious."

As the mayor, she understood the weight of her impartiality, the importance of each smile and nod as she sampled the contestants' heartfelt efforts. With spoon in hand, she moved from one entry to the next, her taste buds alighting with flavors both bold and subtle. Her words were measured, her praises genuine but evenly distributed, ensuring no hint of favoritism clouded the spirited competition. In each spoonful, she tasted not just the ingredients but the love and pride of her community.

As the day's celebrations continued around her, Reva reflected on her love for Thunder Mountain. From her unexpected role as the town's mayor to her newfound passion for skeet shooting, Thunder Mountain had embraced her, and she had embraced the town in return.

Upon graduating from high school, she'd left Thunder Mountain to pursue a prestigious education at Tulane University, after which the allure of high-powered law firms in New York, Chicago, and Los Angeles beckoned her with promises of success, wealth, and prestige. She could have had it all, but she chose to return to this small, tight-knit community in Wyoming, and she never looked back.

In Reva's mind, success was not solely defined by external recognition or a hefty bank account. True accomplishment was about making a difference in the lives of the people you cared about and being a part of something greater than yourself.

Thunder Mountain meant more to her than just the picturesque backdrop found on postcards in Dorothy Vaughn's Bear Country Gift Store. It was the heart of her existence, a place where her roots ran deep. She'd grown up in this mountain town and four of her best school friends had remained close. They were her tribe.

Charlie Grace was a single mom who owned and operated the Teton Trails Guest Ranch, an enterprise she opened just last spring. After a rocky start, the ranch was now thriving—as was her relationship with both her father and her new guy friend, Nick Thatcher.

Lila and her teenage daughter lived at the other end of town. Like Charlie Grace, she was raising a daughter on her own. Six months into her pregnancy, her husband of less than a year tragically died in a helicopter crash in Fallujah.

Lila currently worked with Doc Tillman down at the veterinary clinic, which was perfect given her love of anything soft and furry. Despite all that she juggled, Lila returned to school via an online program from the University of Colorado to pursue a large animal veterinarian license with a specialty in horses. "Camille's college fund needs a bit of help," she claimed. "I need the money the extra certification will provide." Never mind the fact that she was nearly killing herself in the process.

Capri Jacobs still lived with her parents. When questioned about the decision, she shrugged. "It's free." The rest of them knew full well that cash did not weigh in as the deciding factor. Capri owned Grand Teton Whitewater Adventures. She killed it financially, especially during the heavy tourist season. Her chosen profession also left her available in the winters when she alternated filling her time with binging seasons of *Gilmore Girls* on television and snowmobile racing on the local circuit.

Wild adventures aside, Capri dedicated herself to taking care of her mother and stepdad, a man who thankfully traded in his affinity for bourbon and replaced it with lemonade several years back. Sadly, Dick now fought a cancer diagnosis.

Reva's girlfriends had become the pillars of her life, the steady constants, especially after her split with Merritt. No matter what else demanded their attention, they gathered weekly over drinks and dinner, sharing their joys and struggles. As the years passed and she never married or had a family of her own, their importance grew even more profound. These girls were her air. Without them, she wouldn't be able to breathe.

Sure, there were moments of loneliness that crept in, most often when she saw families thriving. A deep place in her heart that longed to be a wife and mother was a companion she couldn't quite outgrow.

"So, what do you say? You want to head out to the ranch and share the news with Charlie Grace and Lila?" Capri asked, her voice breaking into Reva's mental reverie.

Reva looped arms with her close friend. There was no reason to tarnish her day with melancholy. Instead, she'd focus on how her life was richly blessed with the love and camaraderie of these extraordinary women, and so much more. Like they said in her weekly meetings, gratitude helps you fall in love with the life you already have.

"Good plan," she said, grinning. "I can't think of anyone I'd rather celebrate my tournament loss with."

Want more?

www.kelliecoatesgilbert.com/books

ABOUT THE AUTHOR

USA Today Bestselling Author Kellie Coates Gilbert has won readers' hearts with her heartwarming and highly emotional stories about women and the relationships that define their lives. As a former legal investigator, Kellie brings a unique blend of insight and authenticity to her stories, ensuring that readers are hooked from the very first page.

Born and raised amidst the breathtaking beauty of Sun Valley, Idaho, Kellie draws inspiration from the vibrant landscapes of her youth, infusing her stories with a vivid sense of place. Kellie now lives with her husband of over thirty-five years in Dallas, where she spends most days by her pool drinking sweet tea and writing the stories of her heart.

Learn more about Kellie and her books at www.kelliecoatesgilbert.com

Enjoy special discounts by buying direct from Kellie at www.kelliecoatesgilbertbooks.com

Sign up for her newsletter and be the first to hear about new releases, sales, news, and VIP-only specials. Click here to sign up: VIP READER NEWS

WHERE TO FIND ME:

Kellie Coates Gilbert's Shop
(Enjoy special discounts!)

Kellie's Website

She's Reading with Kellie Coates Gilbert
GILBERT GIRLS - Readers Group
(Facebook groups)

Made in the USA
Monee, IL
29 January 2025

11224677R10132